SCHOOL
OF THE
DEAD

Other books by Avi

SCHOOL

OF THE

DEAD

AVI

HARPER

An Imprint of HarperCollinsPublishers

Library of Congress Control Number: 2015958397

ISBN 978-0-06-174085-5

Typography by Aurora Parlagreco

16 17 18 19 20   CG/RRDH   10 9 8 7 6 5 4 3 2

First Edition

For Vicki and Steve Palmquist

The first time Uncle Charlie came to live with us he was alive. The second time he came, he was dead.

Uncle Charlie was my mother's uncle, an eighty-something bachelor who I saw only at Baltimore family gatherings: Thanksgiving, Christmas, and Easter. The men wore suits, button-down shirts, and ties. Uncle Charlie always came wearing a frayed checkered shirt, red suspenders, khakis, and worn loafers with tassels. What's more, his clothing was generally rumpled, and not very clean.

A small guy with a lean face, pug nose, and gloomy eyes, he didn't exactly party. More often than not, he sat alone in a corner, listening intently to the chatter while clasping and unclasping his small, bony hands, but not saying much. When people asked him how he was doing, he'd talk vaguely about some group he'd just joined or the strange book he'd recently read, like *Anglo-Saxon Magic* or *The Egyptian Art of Death*. People tended to leave him alone.

When he did *not* show up at those outings, I'd hear adults

saying, "Any news about Uncle Charlie?"

"Don't ask" was the usual reply, along with a shaking of heads, smirks, and a rolling of eyes.

In other words, compared to the rest of my family, Uncle Charlie was different. Maybe that's why I always sensed that there was stuff going on inside him—you know, locked-up, secretive stuff. Not that I ever saw him *do* anything unusual.

Though my cousins and I kept our distance, at some point one of us would usually whisper, "What's the deal with Uncle Charlie?"

Took a while, but I found out.

It all began during a family Christmas gathering. After the big dinner, with people hanging around doing not much, I noticed Uncle Charlie, as usual, sitting off by himself. Except he was staring at me. I had no idea why. Then I realized he was beckoning me over.

Puzzled—we rarely talked—I went up to him.

At first, all he did was gaze intently at me with his unhappy eyes until, in a croaky voice, he said, "You're Tony, right? Ellie's son."

"Uh-huh."

"Glad to see you." He held out a small hand, the narrow fingers crooked and sort of clawlike. Not knowing what else to do, I shook. He was kind of weak.

"What grade are you in?" he asked.

"Sixth."

"Perfect," he said, some light coming to his eyes, along with a sly smile. Not only was it rare for Uncle Charlie to smile, but this was an *I know something you don't know* smile. Having no idea what it meant, or how to respond, I backed away. Even so, during the next few hours he kept glancing at me. It made me uncomfortable.

Why should Uncle Charlie care about me?

It was during our long drive back home to Connecticut that I said to my parents, "How come Uncle Charlie is so weird?"

Dad snorted. "Every family has at least one weird uncle."

My parents exchanged looks, and then Mom said, "You might as well know: He's moving in with us."

"You're kidding. Uncle Charlie? *Why?*"

Mom said, "He lost his apartment, his health is poor—he has a heart problem—and he's old. He needs to be with family."

"What happened to his apartment?"

"Evicted," said Dad.

Mom shot a sharp look at Dad, as if saying *You weren't supposed to say that*, but I caught it and said, "How come he was evicted?"

Dad, warned, said only, "It's not clear."

"Okay, but why is he coming to *us*?"

"We had a family meeting," Mom explained. "You know, your uncles, aunts, adult cousins. Since your dad and I have jobs that keep us late so often, meaning you're home so much alone, the idea is that it might be good for you—and him—if he moved in with us."

Dad said, "We do have that spare bedroom at the back of our house."

Mom added, "He's actually fairly well off, has his own car and health insurance. To be brutally honest, Tony, I don't think Uncle Charlie has long to live. That heart. The main point: He *is* family. Inviting him to move in is the decent thing to do. It's hard to be old and facing death alone."

I worried about what it was going to be like having Uncle Charlie live with us. Would I have to take care of him? Why had he been so curious about me? What was that secretive smile all about? And . . . what was it like for him to be facing death?

A couple of weeks later, Uncle Charlie moved in.

Now, I have to admit that once Uncle Charlie was around, my feelings about him changed. Because he had changed. He was clean, neat, wore regular clothing. He smiled, had energy, and was happy to talk about lots of things, interesting things.

I did *not* have to take care of him. Just the opposite. Within a month of his coming, I stopped minding that my parents worked late so often. When it happened, I went to Uncle Charlie for what I needed: driving me places, getting things. I listened to his stories and his jokes, which he told a lot. I got the dinners *I* wanted—mac and cheese, pizza, hamburgers, fries, ice cream. If I needed advice—school, friends—Uncle Charlie gave it. In other words, he turned out to be a cool guy. Of course, sometimes when we'd go somewhere, he'd suddenly stand very still and gasp, "Hold it!" trying to catch his breath. When he finally did, he'd just grin and say, "Not dead yet."

When I asked him, "Uncle Charlie, how come you're so different from the way you used to be?"

"Tony," he said, "it meant a lot that your folks invited me here. At my age, it isn't fun being alone. But you know what the best thing about living here is? *You.* I love being with kids. You, most of all. For an old guy like me, it's like having a new life."

Okay, life. But the thing was, it hadn't taken long for me to realize that it wasn't *this* life that interested Uncle Charlie. What fascinated him was the *next* life, what he called "the other side."

As we got to know each other, Uncle Charlie told me wild

stories about things that had happened to him, stories not even my mom—his niece—knew. How he had traveled to out-of-the-way places like Nepal, Tasmania, and Chiapas, where he'd had bizarre adventures living with mystics, fakirs, and shamans. He told me about near-death experiences. Talking to spirits. "Of course," he added, "things can get a bit out of control. Neighbors complain."

"Is that how come you got evicted?"

"Who told you about that?" he asked, slipping in that sly smile of his.

I grinned.

"Oh," he said, "some friends and I were trying to talk to . . . the other side. Our meeting became a little—what do you kids say?—rowdy. No big deal."

If there was one thing in the world I hated, it was *fake*. High on my hate list were adults who faked enjoying doing kids' stuff. But Uncle Charlie *loved* kids' stuff. He and I spent hours playing video games filled with wizards, vampires, and warlocks. We watched TV shows about ghosts and phantoms. He read me spooky stories by Poe, Stevenson, and Lovecraft, his croaky voice making them really eerie.

When I got home from school, we might even go to the shabby theater he'd somehow discovered, which showed old black-and-white movies about the supernatural, like *Night of the Living Dead.* After those films, we'd go to what became Uncle Charlie's favorite store, the Witch's Basement. I had no idea how he'd found it, but the store was packed with fantasy books, games, and costumes—Halloween every day of the year.

It was fun.

One day Uncle Charlie said, "Tony, when I die, I really want you to *join* me." His eyes brightened when he said it, and he had that sly look I'd come to love, which I took to mean he was just joking.

Without much thought, I said, "Sure."

In fact, the more he talked about ghosts and supernatural stuff, the more ordinary they seemed. For instance: When my friends came around, Uncle Charlie asked them about their relatives—if they were about to die, or, if they had died, how and when, natural causes or accidents.

"How come he talks about death all the time?" my friend Mike asked. "It's odd."

"He knows that he's going to die soon," I told Mike. "So he likes to joke that he's just going to move somewhere else."

I told Uncle Charlie, "Mike thinks you're odd."

Uncle Charlie laughed and said, "He's right. But I never get even. I get odder."

That made me laugh.

Then my friend Bill came over, and when Uncle Charlie learned that Bill's aunt had recently died, he decided we should go to "the other side" and talk to her spirit. He darkened his room, burned incense, played eerie music, made us hold hands, and spoke strange words. In the middle of it, Uncle Charlie got all gaspy and out of breath. It was bad, as if he was really about to go to the other side right then. So of course we never talked to Bill's aunt.

Even so, Mom got a call from Bill's mother.

"Tony's great-uncle," she said, "really upset Bill by trying to talk to his late aunt."

I heard Mom—who knew nothing about it—say, "My old uncle Charlie is with us because he has health problems. The good thing is, with my husband's and my work schedules, he does look after Tony. And Tony really enjoys his company."

Trouble was, Bill and Mike—and other friends—stopped coming over because of Uncle Charlie. They said he was too creepy. When I told my friends about things he had done, they started calling *me* "weirdo." Hating that, I hung out just with Uncle Charlie more than ever.

In April, when I turned twelve, Uncle Charlie gave me the coolest birthday present: a red Gibbon slackline.

A slackline is a nylon tape, two inches wide, stretched some distance, not quite like a tightrope but bowed. You get on it—not easy—and set one foot before the other. You stand on it, trying to keep your balance, swaying, adjusting, and trying to find your center. Then you try to move forward, or back—if you can.

He also gave me a book called *Walk the Line*. On the first page it read:

WARNING.
Take responsibility for your own actions as they pertain to slackline. Slackline can be dangerous, resulting in injury or possibly death.

The guy who wrote the book, Scott Balcom, did some insane walks across canyons, so I guess he knew what he was talking about.

My parents would never have given me a slackline—too risky.

Uncle Charlie was enthusiastic. "When you walk the slackline, you're not in the air; you're not on the ground. Sort of half alive, half dead. Good practice for being a ghost."

I said, "I don't believe in ghosts."

He laughed. "You will, someday."

"Someday?"

"When people say *someday*, it's like making a wish."

All I can say is that when I was on the slackline, I didn't think about ghosts. I just loved trying to walk it.

After Uncle Charlie had been living with us for a few months, he came up with a huge idea: we should all move to San Francisco, where he grew up. Seems he wanted me to go to the Penda School, a private K–8 school he went to when he was a kid. "Tony will get a better education than he gets here," he told us.

My parents, who had become bored with their jobs—Mom in marketing, Dad a civil engineer—talked about moving. Dad said, "Who wouldn't want to live in San Francisco?" And Mom wanted more challenging work. I reminded them that I had stopped liking my school. And Uncle Charlie kept talking about how great the Penda School was.

In the end, my folks decided that if they found better positions out there, we could go. It took a while, but then they announced that both of them had landed great jobs in San Francisco. We would move early October.

Uncle Charlie was thrilled. "Now," he said, "we just have to get you into Penda."

Mom got in touch with the Penda School, only to be told

that it was full. Still, they said I'd be wait-listed because there could always be a change.

Wanting to get to a place where I could make new friends, I was disappointed. Dad said, "I'm sure San Francisco has lots of good schools."

And Uncle Charlie—sly smile in place—said, "Maybe I can help."

The very next night—my folks were working late again— Uncle Charlie said something new to me.

"Know why I was willing to move here?"

"So you wouldn't be alone."

"Nope. I wanted to get to know *you*. And because I wanted you to go to the Penda School."

"What's so special about it?"

He thought a moment and then said, "Kindergarten to eighth grade. And it's . . . full of life."

I thought of asking him, Which life? This one or the next? I didn't.

I should have.

Two weeks after my parents decided we would all move to San Francisco, Uncle Charlie became ill. Feverish. Weak. Numbness in his hands. So right after school I would zip on home, measure out his meds, do his errands, and sometimes feed him. I even helped him get into his blue pajamas and to bed in his room.

Then this awful thing happened.

It was a warm night in late June. My folks were working late, so I was alone with Uncle Charlie. Telling me he had painful tightness in his chest and a general chill, he took to bed. I sat in a chair by his side. After a while, the book he had been reading, *Cults of the Caribbean*, fell to the floor. Gradually, his eyes closed.

Not sure if he was sleeping, I stayed put. The increasing humidity made my skin feel crawly. Outside, the wind began to whip and whistle. Treetops started to sway. The air became heavy, the room dim. Window curtains fluttered.

I fell into a doze, only to awaken with a start. Uncle Charlie had reached out and gripped my hand with his skinny fingers.

"Hey, Tony," he whispered in that cloggy voice of his.

I looked around.

"Have I convinced you that ghosts are real?" he rasped.

I muttered. "Not . . . really."

"They are," he said. "Believe me."

"I do," I said for his sake, while letting him cling to my hand. He was trembling.

Loud thunder drew near. Rain tapped the side of the house, sounding like tiny feet running up and down the walls. The air in the room began to swirl in slow circles.

Uncle Charlie had been lying very still, when his grip on my hand tightened. "Tony, I'm going to die."

Scared, having no idea what to do or say, I just mumbled, "Hope not."

"How about coming with me to the other side?"

"What?"

He shifted his head slightly so he could look at me. For a second his eyes brightened. "Know what Albert Einstein said?"

I shook my head.

"'The distinction between past, present, and future is only an illusion.'"

"I don't get it."

"Remember the number seven."

"What about seven?"

"The most important number in the universe. Means there's a way you and I can stay together. When I go, I really want you to join me. It's not *that* hard to do. Just respect the past and protect the future."

Sure he was becoming confused, all I said was, "If you say so."

"Tony," he went on, his voice weaker, "your seventh-grade year is going to be big."

He gave my hand another squeeze, sighed deeply—sort of a raspy hiss—and said, "Here we go. Trust me."

His small, bony hand continued to hold on, and his eyes remained open—as if watching me—but he died.

Outside, the storm erupted.

Being alone when Uncle Charlie died was ghastly. The burial service, on a hot and humid day, was almost as bad. It was held in a funeral parlor with fake wood–paneled walls and piped-in, gooey organ music that a snail would have found slow. Since the cooling system was busted, the air reeked with something that smelled like burnt sugar, meant to hide—I was sure—the stink of death. The quiet was so deep I kept hearing the prickly rustle of clothing, the shifting of feet, and the clearing of throats. It made my skin crawl. Then there was a long sermon preached by an old minister friend of Uncle Charlie's, something sappy about souls set free to wander.

The worst was seeing Uncle Charlie in an open casket, looking like a wax doll with rouged cheeks. The undertakers had closed his eyes, which had been so full of fun.

As far as I was concerned, I had lost my best friend.

Uncle Charlie was buried in a local cemetery, the muddle of crosses looking like a forest of crooked trees. When we reached the open grave, it even began to rain. Two shaggy-haired gravediggers stood off to one side, leaning on their spades. They were wearing red gloves.

Uncle Charlie was the first person I really knew who passed on. I understood nothing about death. Hadn't really thought about it, much less gotten it. All I knew was that when his casket was lowered into the grave, it felt as if a part of me was buried too.

Weeks went by. Despite all Uncle Charlie's jokey talk of ghosts, the supernatural, and *the other side*, I wasn't prepared for his death. Moreover, the summer was hot and humid and I had lost my friends. I felt abandoned. Sort of like wandering in a fog. With my folks still at their old jobs, I was alone tons of time. I spent hours walking my red slackline, which was hooked up in our backyard.

Mom did not approve. "It's vacation time. You should be out playing and doing things with kids, not staying home by yourself like a circus performer without an audience."

But walking the line made me feel good. It was my way of keeping Uncle Charlie's memory alive.

One sticky night when my parents were not home, and it was so steamy I felt as if I were wearing five turtleneck wool sweaters, I snuck into Uncle Charlie's old room. I found some of his incense, lit it, played his strange music, and tried to say the mixed-up words he'd used when attempting to contact my friend's dead aunt. I wanted to get to the other side and talk to Uncle Charlie. All I heard were twilight crickets, creaking like a door that never fully opened.

How stupid could I be? I should have accepted what I had always known was true: Uncle Charlie's supernatural talk was just a joke.

At least, that was what I told myself.

But since I couldn't get Uncle Charlie out of my mind, my parents took me to a psychologist. Her report: "Your son, Anthony Gilbert, was deeply disturbed by his uncle Charlie's death. He's depressed."

"What's wrong with thinking about Uncle Charlie?" I asked Dad. "And what's *depressed* mean?"

He said, "It's like being half dead."

When I remained sad, not happy with anything, my parents kept reminding me we were about to move to San Francisco in the fall.

Dad kept saying, "New jobs for us. Cool new school for you."

"That is," Mom cautioned, "if you can get in. Hope there's space."

Then I had to start back in my old school. Mid-September in the middle of packing for the move to San Francisco—we were told that the Penda School, the very place Uncle Charlie had wanted me to go, could enroll me as soon as I could get there. They would hold a place.

Delighted, my parents found an apartment near the school. That's why, October 5, a Sunday morning, the three of us were on the sidewalk, looking at the Penda School for the first time.

And that's when Uncle Charlie showed up again.

He looked exactly the way he had at those family gatherings: a small, old guy with a lean, pug-nosed face, dressed in a frayed checkered shirt, suspenders, torn jeans, and, yes, those tasseled loafers. A couple of differences: his eyes were bright, and he was smiling at me.

Let me make it clear: I did *not* believe in ghosts. I simply told myself that Uncle Charlie and I had spent so much time together, talked so much, done so many things, and had such fun, that I had never stopped thinking about him.

In other words, as far as I was concerned, I was not *seeing* Uncle Charlie. I was seeing my *memory* of him.

Think about memory. You can't slice a memory like a loaf of bread, but you can smell it, taste it, and see it, right? Even though memories can't talk to you, memories are real. It was his idea that had brought us to San Francisco. I was standing by the school he'd wanted me to attend. How could I *not* remember him?

Of course, my parents didn't see him. Uncle Charlie was *my* memory.

The main thing was, seeing him made me happy. I felt it would be great to have him around to help me in my new city, new home, and new school. What's more, I figured I'd need his help, because the Penda School was not like any school I had ever seen before.

The Penda School sat atop San Francisco's Pacific Heights, half a block wide and two stories high. It was built of dark red wood; massive stone steps led to double doors with thick glass I couldn't see through. There were multiple steep-pitched roofs, linked by a spiderweb of crests. There were gray slate shingles, bulky redbrick chimneys, plus tall windows bracketed by posts and moldings. It also had four towers, the tallest much higher than the others. Topping that tower was a weather vane.

Though the building appeared to be more than a hundred

years old, right next to it was a gigantic tree, higher than the big tower. The tree had to be even older than the school. The school reminded me of the haunted houses in those ghost movies I'd seen with Uncle Charlie. "That building," I said to him, "is totally fake."

Of course I didn't expect an answer, but I was happy when he just offered that sly smile of his.

Dad, however, assumed I was talking to him. "It's anything but fake," he said. He opened the brochure the school had sent us and read:

The Penda School came into existence in 1897, when Mrs. Penda, a wealthy widow who owned redwood forests in Northern California, established the school soon after her only child, a boy, died. So great was her grief that shortly afterward she too passed away. All the same, she left her mansion and an endowment for a boys' and girls' school so that they might "Respect the past and protect the future."

Mom, smiling, said, "So make sure, Tony, in school, to show a healthy respect for history, and protect the future."

Remembering that "Respect the past and protect the future" was something Uncle Charlie had told me, I asked him, "Protect *who* from *what*?"

All Mom said was, "Just a motto. I wouldn't worry about it."

I took the brochure from Dad and flipped through it. It was stuffed with pictures of laughing, hugging students. "That's so fake," I said.

"Do you know how often you say *fake*?" said Mom.

"Do you know how many things *are* fake?"

Pointing to the school's highest tower, I said to Uncle Charlie, "Do they have classes up there?"

"Astronomy," suggested Mom.

"Religion," offered Dad. "Because I'll bet that weather vane on top is Gabriel."

I said, "Who's Gabriel?"

"A big-time angel. See his trumpet? His job is to announce the end of the world with a toot of his horn. When he does, all the dead arise."

There's a lot of death attached to this school, I thought as I stared at the building and said, "It's . . . weird."

"Nowadays," said Dad, "*weird* means 'strange.' Know what the word used to mean?"

"No."

"*Fate.*"

"Whose?" I asked Uncle Charlie.

Dad said, "Yours, I guess." And he laughed.

So did Uncle Charlie, silently.

"Just remember," said Mom, "Uncle Charlie left money so you could come to this school. You heard him say how much he loved it when he went."

To which Dad added, "Just don't try to live up to Uncle Charlie's expectations. Accept the fact that he's gone and you're on your own. But—no harm in enjoying the fact that he went here."

"Think the school is still good?" I asked Uncle Charlie.

Mom said, "I guess that's why he wanted you to come here."

Dad added, "We were lucky they found a place for you."

"How'd that happen?" I asked Uncle Charlie.

The old guy gave his biggest grin yet, but it was Mom who said, "I gather someone suddenly left. And maybe Uncle Charlie put in a word."

"Does the school know I'm related?" I asked Uncle Charlie.

Dad shook his head. "We didn't tell them, and with your different last names, they won't know. You're here on your own."

Mom, not thrilled by how much I still went on about Uncle Charlie, said, "Let's get some frozen yogurt."

Dad used his phone to tap in a search. "Yogurt place right down the hill."

I said, "Everything is downhill in San Francisco."

As we started off, Mom put an arm around my shoulder. I shrugged her off and looked back. Uncle Charlie had disappeared, but I saw the face of a girl—at least I thought it was a girl—staring out at me from one of the school's first-floor windows. "Do they have school on weekends?" I asked.

"Doubt it," said Dad.

I said, "There's a girl looking out."

"Really?" said Mom, turning. By the time she looked, the girl's face was gone.

"Maybe not," I had to admit. Even so, I looked at the school again. Not seeing anyone, I gazed higher, to the window in the tallest tower. Another face was there, a boy with blond curly hair. He was also staring at me. At least he was until he too vanished.

I thought, *Weird.*

Which naturally made me think about what Dad had just said about the word *weird*: that it didn't just mean "strange" but also "fate."

Turned out he had it right—both ways.

My first day at Penda—Monday the sixth—was to begin at eight thirty. Before my alarm buzzed at seven thirty, I was yanked from restless sleep by a sharp crack of lightning.

Bolting up in bed, I listened as thunder and rain lashed against our apartment building. It reminded me of the night Uncle Charlie died.

I flipped my pillow to the cool side, drew up my blanket, and lay back. When I had asked Uncle Charlie why he wanted me to go to the Penda School, all he'd said was, "It's . . . full of life." So, not knowing much about the Penda School, I was uneasy.

A private school: Would the kids be snobby rich? Was it going to be hard? Would I have to play a sport? Would I have any friends? I suppose my worries explain why I hadn't unpacked my junk yet—as if I might go back east.

Like a good memory, Uncle Charlie was standing at the foot of my bed, eyes full of fun.

I said, "You wanted me to go here, so it's going to be okay, right?"

He offered a smile and faded away.

Reassured, I got up. Still, what I really wanted to do was walk my slackline. I had strung it up in my room from my closet door to the bureau. But I knew I had to go to school.

Over my desk chair Mom had laid out my new clothes: ironed tan pants and a white collared shirt, along with one of Dad's red-and-blue-striped ties. The Penda School had a dress code.

Once dressed, I joined my parents for breakfast in the small kitchen. Nodding toward the storm, I asked, "How am I going to get to school?"

"Usually, you'll walk," said Mom. "But we'll take a cab today. Showing up soaked on your first day would look odd."

I said, "Uncle Charlie once told me he didn't get even. Just odder."

Mom patted my hand. "Now that we're in San Francisco, how about some cheerful thoughts?"

"I like remembering him," I said, and turned to my oatmeal and raisins.

Dad punched out a number on his smartphone. "We'd like a cab." He gave our address and looked a question at Mom.

She answered, "Twenty minutes."

Into the phone, Dad said, "Twenty minutes."

Mom said, "Your dad and I will be at work, so at the end of the day you'll need to walk home by yourself. Okay?"

I said, "Uncle Charlie will come with me."

Mom, exasperated, said, "Tony, Uncle Charlie is no longer with us."

"For you, maybe." I pushed my empty bowl away and gulped some milk. "I don't ever intend to forget him."

Dad said, "Let me do your tie."

I stood before him.

Dad said, "Nervous?"

"No," I lied.

"You'll have a great future there," said Mom.

"'The distinction between past, present, and future is only an illusion.'"

"Where'd *that* come from?"

"Albert Einstein. One of the last things Uncle Charlie said to me."

Mom sighed. "For the present, please get ready."

I grabbed my empty backpack, flung in my cell phone, and was ready to start at the Penda School.

As Mom and I stood inside the apartment-building lobby waiting for the cab, Uncle Charlie looked on.

"You coming to school with me?" I asked him.

Mom said, "I'll make sure you're settled. Then I'll have to get to work."

The taxi pulled up. As if to announce its arrival, there was another leap of lightning. Rain strafed the pavement.

Mom, her umbrella open, said, "Go!"

I ran to the cab, yanked the door open, and jumped in. Mom followed, swiveled to close down the umbrella, got in, and slammed the door.

"Penda School," she said to the driver, who, already tapping into his meter, looked around. "I know. Only six blocks but you'll get a good tip. It's this young man's first day."

"What about lunch?" I asked Mom.

"There's a school cafeteria. We were told it's good."

"School food always sucks."

"Someday you might actually *like* something."

"Uncle Charlie said people used the word *someday* like it was a wish."

"Tony, please . . . Uncle Charlie is just a memory."

"Exactly," I said. The window on my side being steamy, I rubbed it clear and peeked out. Uncle Charlie was standing across the street, watching and smiling. I gave him a quick thumbs-up.

The cab ride was very short.

I looked out at Uncle Charlie. "Thanks for coming," I told him.

"You're welcome," Mom said, and reached out to smooth my hair and adjust my tie. "You're going to love it."

I said, "People in marketing want everybody to love everything."

Mom muttered something, handed seven bucks to the cabbie, unlatched the door, poked her umbrella out, opened it with a snap, and stepped from the car. I messed my hair, pulled my tie crooked, and followed. Outside, I paused to gaze at the school. The rain had turned its redwood siding the color of dark blood.

I must have looked like a new kid, because a few polite students held the main doors open for us.

"Here we go," said Mom as we went in.

To which I replied, "That's what Uncle Charlie said right before he died."

We stepped into an enormous reception hall. No cement-block walls painted tan and plastered with NO BULLYING! posters. No school-spirit streamers. No kids' bad art. No bulky display cases full of fake silver trophies or soft footballs with winning scores stenciled in white.

Instead, walls were paneled with fancy dark wood, each section framed by carved moldings. A tiled floor of deep sea blue was covered by a water-absorbing red carpet. The carpet made me think of a scab. In one corner stood a clump of potted plants with large glossy leaves, a reminder of long-gone summers.

In my old school, kids charged in as if it were pizza-giveaway day. Here the kids were quiet, self-controlled, like at a school dance with too many chaperones. Overhead, a large chandelier was hanging from a high ceiling, its million glass bits shivering like a delicate wind chime.

The hall extended to a place I couldn't see. But forty feet in, left and right, were massive, matching curved stairways. Built wide like a wrestler's arms, the steps met at the second floor. Right under where the steps joined, brass letters proclaimed: RESPECT THE PAST—PROTECT THE FUTURE.

Though that was what Uncle Charlie had said to me, I still didn't understand it. The school was so quiet, so plush, I was reminded of that funeral parlor where Uncle Charlie's service had been held.

Mom moved me toward a door that said SCHOOL OFFICE. As she opened it, she whispered, "Try to look as if you're glad to be here."

She must have read my mind, because by then I was already thinking, *This school* is *weird*.

The school office was a room cut in half by a long counter and desk. Walls were fine wood, the deep carpet golf-course green, the air smelling like fake pine air.

Sitting behind the desk was an elderly woman clutching a landline phone in her knuckle-knobbed hand. Her thin, gray, and straggly hair and wrinkled face and neck made her look as if she had been roosting behind that desk for a hundred years. Either she was using eye shadow, or she had trouble sleeping. Her thin white lips grimaced while saying into the phone, "Thanks for calling, Ms. Morris. I'm sure Emma will be better soon."

The second she hung up, another call rang.

"So sorry," the woman said to us, and took up the phone again.

I gazed about the room. A big leather-covered couch—like a partially deflated rhinoceros—stood against one wall. On a nearby table, maybe a hundred school yearbooks were neatly lined up, the dates on their spines reminding me of a row of tombstones. School brochures were spread out in a fan.

On the wall over the table was a huge gold-framed painting of an old lady sitting in a bulky, throne-like chair. Her fierce, dark-eyed, jut-chinned face was long and narrow with high cheekbones. Her lips were tight and pale. Black hair was piled atop her head, while her neck was encased in a stiff collar. Black-gloved hands were clutching armrests. It was as if the chair were plunging down and the old girl was not happy about where she was headed.

Finding the image unsettling, I turned away. On the opposite wall hung another large framed painting. This one was of a boy—maybe twelve years old like me—with blond curly hair. His jacket and trousers were dark green. A white lace collar circled his neck like a fancy noose. His shoes were high-buttoned and polished. His hands were by his sides, balled in tense, tight fists.

But what really held my attention were the boy's pale face and eyes, eyes full of dread, as if something awful was coming right at him. And oddly, I had the sensation I'd seen him before.

Not that I could recall where.

The woman at the desk hung up her phone and with sarcasm thick as old pancake syrup said, "Forgive me: bad weather, sick children. May I help you?"

Mom pulled me from the boy's painting. "I'm Ellie Gilbert," she said. "This is Anthony, my son. He's starting school today."

For a moment the woman stared at me with great intensity, until her face abruptly softened. "Oh yes, Tony Gilbert. Of course. Our new student. Welcome to the Penda School," she said, as if embarrassed by her first reception. "We're *so* glad you're here. I'm Mrs. Zabalink, or Mrs. Z, as the young people have been calling me for more years than I wish to count. Dear me, what a day to begin. I assure you, storms like this are so rare in San Francisco."

Abruptly, she stopped talking and went back to considering me as if I were a specimen on a dissecting table.

Breaking the awkward silence, Mom said, "I guess Tony needs to get to class."

Mrs. Z yanked back to life. "Forgive me. I'm sure you're eager. But Ms. Foxton, school head, likes to welcome new students. This way, please. She's expecting you."

I hated school officials. Back in Connecticut, after Uncle Charlie died, they'd had only two things to say to me: "Lighten up." "Smile." Fake cheer by the garbage-truckful.

Mrs. Z guided us into a large office with a fireplace on one side, full of fake logs. Antique-looking wooden file cabinets stood against the opposite wall. Each drawer had brass numbers for a span of years—the earliest 1897—up to the current year. Sitting on one cabinet was a red plastic flashlight. I liked that. Plastic is honest fake.

Against another wall was a long, low, and narrow wooden chest, its elaborately carved side toward me. I was sure it was empty. Fake again. Over the chest was a framed list: FORMER SCHOOL HEADS. The long list suggested *heads* didn't stay on for long.

On the wall behind the large desk was a photograph of joyful kids, probably models. Three empty chairs sat before the desk. Their emptiness was real. Behind the desk sat Ms. Foxton, the school head. As we walked in, she stood, smiled, came around, and held out a hand.

I was surprised by how young she was, trim and healthy, with brown hair tied off behind her neck, ponytail fashion, and wearing a white blouse, a knee-length green skirt, and polished heels. Everything was in place, including her smile.

"Hello, Tony," she said, "I'm Gloria Foxton. Let me welcome you to the Penda School."

I shook her hand. Ms. Foxton didn't just take my hand; she held it and looked into my eyes as if searching for something. I had no idea what she found in me—but what I saw in her eyes was fear.

Startled, I tried to pull back, but she held on.

"We're so glad you're joining us, Tony," she said, though her eyes said something different.

She let my hand go and went back behind her desk, saying, "Let's sit and talk a moment."

Mom said, "We're grateful you were able to find a place for Tony even though your term has already begun."

"An . . . unexpected student dropout," said Ms. Foxton "A . . . sad story." Her voice had become careful.

I tried to read her eyes, but she kept her focus elsewhere. I followed her gaze. She was looking behind me, at that carved chest.

"Here you are, Tony," she said, and picked up a manila

folder, as if to draw my attention to her. "Your application. It will join the files of hundreds of other Penda students." She gestured toward the cabinets. "Since 1897, we've kept track of each and every student. Some quite illustrious. I gather you're new to San Francisco. May I ask what brought you?"

Mom said, "Job opportunities for my husband and me."

"Congratulations," said Ms. Foxton. Even as I watched, her eyes shifted back to me, and her fear returned.

Blinking to work it away, she continued on: "Before you go to class, there are a few things we should talk over." On she chatted about school requirements, rules, and expectations. Not interested, I kept watching her as she shifted her eyes from my mother, to me, to that chest. I looked at it again. It made me think of Uncle Charlie's casket. In fact, I liked to think of him sitting on the chest, eyes lively with delight. Whatever was making Ms. Foxton fearful, thinking of him was reassuring to me.

"Well now, Tony," said Ms. Foxton, "shall you and I go up to room seven? That's Mr. Batalie's room. He's the seventh-grade homeroom and English teacher. I've printed up your class schedule."

I took it without looking at it.

As Ms. Foxton led us through the outer office, I stopped in

front of the boy's portrait.

"Excuse me," I said, pointing. "Who's that?"

Mrs. Z, the secretary, looked up, but it was Ms. Foxton who said, "That's Mrs. Penda's son. We speak of him fondly as 'the Penda Boy.' It was his death that led his mother to create this school."

Gazing at the painting, I had two thoughts: *Why was he so full of fear?* And again, that puzzling notion that I'd seen him before.

"Of course," said Mrs. Z, "over there, that's Mrs. Penda, the school founder."

I turned. "How come she's so angry?"

Ms. Foxton said, "The portrait was painted right after her boy's death."

To which Mrs. Z added, "Mrs. Penda had been a beautiful woman but—as you can see—she was devastated."

As Ms. Foxton gazed at the portrait, distress oozed back into her eyes. Catching me looking at her, she flipped on her smile and said, "We need to get you to class."

As we went out of the office, she leaned toward me so Mrs. Z couldn't hear: "To be honest," she whispered, "not a painting I would have placed there, but our board of trustees insists."

Which painting did she mean?

❖ ❖ ❖

In the reception hall, Mom shook hands with Ms. Foxton, then gave me a last look while mouthing the words *tie* and *I love you*. Noting her priorities, I watched her head out into the rain. Uncle Charlie, looking at me from a corner, offered a reassuring grin.

"We need to go this way," said Ms. Foxton. She led me up one of the main carpeted stairways, wide enough for us to go side by side. As we walked, I looked around. On the other steps, a boy was also coming up.

For a half second, I thought he was the same boy whose portrait I had just seen in the school office. It was as if he was following me.

Ms. Foxton touched my arm so that I looked around as she said, "Dreadful day, isn't it? But the building is wonderfully snug and tight."

She was right. Penda was extremely quiet, no smells of food, sweat, or old books. And clean. Not a single scrap of paper, dropped jacket, or left backpack. As for that boy, the one on the other steps, he too was gone.

"I gather," said Ms. Foxton as we kept climbing, "your uncle died recently."

"My mom's uncle," I said, wondering how she knew about him.

"Were you close?"

"Yeah," I said.

She became quiet but then said, "Tell me, Tony, do you have a favorite sport?"

"The slackline."

She flicked her fake smile and, ignoring what I said, went on, her voice full of fake energy: "We have the usual team sports here—lacrosse, field hockey, even Ping-Pong. We expect every student to play on one each term. We have clubs too. The Wednesday clubs meet last period. All created by students. You'll get to pick the one you'd like. I'm the track coach and adviser for the International Club. Your teacher Mr. Batalie is the basketball coach and Book Club adviser. Tall as you are, I bet you play basketball."

"Not really."

"Well, I'm sure you can find something you enjoy. Just let Mrs. Z know which team you'd like. She coordinates that from the office. What about academic subjects? Have a favorite?"

"Don't think so."

"What *are* you interested in?"

"Not much."

That capped her chatter. I was glad. I hated fake-talking adults.

❖ ❖ ❖

We reached the second floor, which was as spotless as the first: Wide hallways, wooden walls and doors, thick carpeting. No lockers. A high ceiling with fancy lighting. No signs with paint-dripped letters reading *Beat West*, *Fifth Grade Rules*, or *Miss B's Brilliants*.

As if reading my mind, Ms. Foxton said, "It's sometimes hard to think of this building as a school. Mrs. Penda's will requires us to keep it as it was.

"It did survive the 1906 earthquake. And the many earthquakes we have in San Francisco. One of your teachers, Mr. Bokor—you'll have history with him—has written a book about the building. Fascinating.

"For safety reasons, the towers are sealed off. In fact, we have a strict rule: no one is allowed into them. Serious consequences if you even try."

I recalled the kid I saw in the tower, but not wanting to get anyone in trouble, I said nothing.

At the end of the hall, she halted before a door. Over it, a metal seven was attached. "This is your homeroom. Mr. Batalie's. As I said, he's your English teacher too. Now, let's meet Friday. I like to be sure everything is working for new students."

Just as she was about to knock on the door, she hesitated.

"Tony, there is something I need to tell you." Her voice became guarded. "There's . . . what shall I say . . . a school tradition of teasing new students about the school being haunted, particularly the towers." Her fake smile turned back on. "A bit of out-of-season Halloween. And," she added, "Halloween is very big here. Promise you won't take the stories seriously."

"I won't," I said, trying to decide if she was teasing.

She tapped on the door. Without waiting for an answer, she opened it, and we stepped into classroom seven.

At the front of the class were a big SMART Board and a teacher's desk. On the wall was a sign that read NO PHONE ZONE. Low bookshelves—stuffed with paperbacks—had been placed under the windows. The inside wall had a long corkboard with student work held up with multicolored pushpins. There was also a row of photo portraits.

Scattered around the room were some twenty-five small tables, plus chairs, all occupied by students, at first glance as many girls as boys. As soon as I entered the room, they looked up. So did the teacher—Mr. Batalie, I assumed.

He was an older man, slightly stooped, with a fringe of gray at the back of his bald head. His pale, wrinkled face with red-rimmed eyes reminded me of those goblins hiding under bridges in kids' fairy-tale books.

"Ah! Tony Gilbert, I presume," he said in a voice some-what rough like Uncle Charlie's. Turning to the class, he said, "Seventh graders, let's welcome Tony to the Penda School."

The students lumbered to their feet. They ranged from tall to short, some looking older, others younger, the usual odd-sized mix of seventh graders. They were diverse, but with the dress code they seemed much the same.

The boys looked like me: tan pants, white shirt, and neck-tie. Tie colors varied a lot. Girls had white collared blouses, neck scarves—all colors—and pleated blue skirts. To my eyes, they were all like an L.L.Bean ad.

"Welcome, Tony," they called in ragged chorus. "We're glad you've come to Penda."

Their grins and looks suggested they were curious about me.

"Good job, Sevens," said Ms. Foxton. "Thank you, Mr. Batalie. I'll leave Tony in your hands."

"I appreciate that, Ms. Foxton. Class, be seated."

Ms. Foxton went. The students sat. Feeling as if I were standing outside a party to which I wasn't certain I'd be invited, I peeked around.

That's when I noticed a boy with a mop of curly blond hair sitting between two kids in the far back row. He was staring at me. It took a second to realize he was the same boy I'd seen coming up the steps, the one who looked like the kid in the school office painting. He even had that fright in his eyes.

Just as I was trying to figure out how the boy could have reached the classroom before me, there was a crack of lightning and the room lights went off.

"Whoa!" cried someone.

"Awesome," said another.

The lights flashed back on. "Quite a welcome," said Mr. Batalie. "Okay, Tony, let's find a desk for you today. Except for me, we don't have permanent desks. That way people get to know one another. For starters, take that empty seat . . ." He searched about the room. "Let's see. There's an open one between Jessica Richards—Jessica, raise your hand, please—and Macauly Tarkington. Mac, hand up."

Two kids sitting in the back row did as asked. I looked. That blond, curly-haired kid, the one I thought I'd recognized, had been sitting between them—but he had vanished.

Having no time to think it out, and with everyone's eyes on me, I made my way to the now-empty seat.

"Hi," said the boy Batalie had called Macauly. "Just call me Mac."

On the chubby side, he had brown parted hair and a twitchy smile on a pale, bland face. His necktie was black. When he held out a dimpled pink hand with closely bitten nails, we shook. His grip was as flabby as a dead fish.

From the other side, the girl named Jessica said, "Hi," and looked up at me with big dark eyes. Her long black hair framed a pale, narrow face with high cheekbones and perfectly formed lipstick-red lips, matching the red of her fingernails. Her neck scarf was as black as her hair.

"Jessica," she said, offering a warm smile while shaking my hand firmly. Then, with a quick, flirty flick, she shoved strands of her black hair back behind her ear.

Thinking how pretty she was, I sat down.

Up front, Mr. Batalie said, "Okay. Tony, this is your English class. We're reading *The Old Man and the Sea*. Indeed, I suspect the class is weary of hearing that it's good for young people to know what it feels like to be ancient—like me."

Mac slid his book over. From the other side, Jessica reached across and pointed to a place in the text. Her right hand had a ring. On it were some small black stones. Seven of them. She was also wearing perfume that reminded me of that sweet, musty smell I'd noticed at Uncle Charlie's funeral.

As the class resumed its book discussion, I was glad to be in the back row. Sitting there, I kept trying to match people with names as they were called, trying to scope out who might be a friend. After a while I realized that the wall of photographs was of all the kids in the room. I did notice an open space, as if a picture had been removed.

That made me think about the boy with the curly blond hair. I gazed about the room. He was absolutely not there. But Uncle Charlie was, standing in a corner, watching me. I told myself to stop thinking about him and focus on the class.

But it was hard, because outside, rain continued to whip against the two large windows, as if trying to get in. Though it was blurry, I could make out that huge tree. I watched it dripping like a slowly melting candle.

Batalie had been droning on for a while when a bell rang. Students leaped from their seats. The room became noisy with chatter.

"That's the midmorning recess bell, Tony," Batalie called above the racket.

I wasn't sure what to do.

"Since Tony is new," Mr. Batalie said, "how about Mac and Jessica escort him to the cafeteria."

"Sure," said Jessica, standing up. She was as tall as I was. "Come on."

"We've got twenty minutes," Mac, much shorter, informed me.

The three of us went into the hall, which was full of kids. I was sure a hundred eyes looked me over. I was distracted by Jessica's hand on my arm.

"Cafeteria is in the basement," she said, pointing down the hall. As she walked, I noticed she had a slight limp.

"Where you coming from?" she asked.

"Connecticut."

"I've been to Boston," she said. "That near where you lived?"

"About a hundred miles west. Hartford area."

"I went to Salem, the Witch House. Ever been there?"

"Nope."

"Sort of lame," she said. "Fake ghosts and all."

"Real is better," said Mac, as we headed down steps. "And—"

Jessica gave him a sharp look. He stopped talking and bit the side of a fingernail.

Feeling I needed to say something, I said, "This a good school?"

"Uptight," said Jessica.

"What way?"

"Penda," said Mac, "thinks a lot of itself."

"Everything is supposed to be perfect," agreed Jessica. "So parents can brag."

"Yeah," said Mac. "If anything, you know, bad happens, the rule is: hide it."

I felt obliged to say, *"Does* anything bad happen?"

Jessica said, "Yeah, it does."

I wanted to ask more, but the press of kids around us increased and was too loud.

We reached the lowest level, ripe with the smell of food.

"Different lines," Mac explained. "Drinks, cookies and muffins, yogurt. No soda."

Only then did I realize I had forgotten to bring money. It must have shown on my face because Jessica said, "Don't worry. Parents are billed. Grab what you want." She pointed. "We always sit over there."

Curious as to who *we* were and why they *always* sat in the same place, I got on line. That's when I noticed Uncle Charlie standing next to the checkout lady, looking over the food I took. Since I hadn't been thinking of him, I wondered why he was there.

After helping myself to a thick-top chocolate-chip muffin and a carton of apple juice, I looked around, not sure where to go. For a second, I thought I noticed that blond boy again, his fearful eyes fixed on me. Simultaneously, I saw Jessica raise her hand across the room.

I worked my way through the crowd and grabbed a chair from an empty table—no one was sitting at either of the ones nearby—and sat down. Aside from Mac and Jessica, there was another boy. Like Mac, he was wearing a black tie.

Jessica gestured to him. "Barney, in our class, right? Tony, the new Seven."

Barney had untidy reddish hair, freckles, and stick-out ears. A pile of sunflower seeds lay in front of him. He would pop one into his mouth, make little nibbling motions with his lips, and then spit out the husks, like a chipmunk. All the while, he considered me with gray, watery eyes.

"Hi," I said, struck by how much older Jessica looked compared to these boys.

There was an awkward silence until Barney leaned forward and whispered, "We're the ones who can tell you what's really happening around here."

Jessica snapped him a hard look. He slunk down. Whatever *they* were, she was in charge.

No one spoke for a moment until Mac said, "Hey, Tony, how come you picked this school?"

"Long story."

Jessica said, "Someone close to you died, right?"

Startled, I said, "How'd you know?"

She smiled. "I smell it on you."

Not sure what to say, I sucked up my juice.

Barney broke the silence. "You play sports?"

"Not much," I said. "What's the school good at?"

The kids looked at one another, as if unsure how to answer. Jessica said, "Building your résumé."

Another pause.

"What music do you like?" Mac asked me.

"Not really into music."

Jessica said, "What are you into?"

I shrugged. "Don't know."

"Cool," said Jessica. "It's what you don't know that's interesting."

"Like weird history," said Barney.

I said, "What's . . . *weird* history?"

Jessica said, "What you'd expect from a school that happened because a kid died."

I must have looked baffled, because Mac said, "You know. The Penda Boy."

I said, "Oh, right."

Jessica touched my arm with her ring hand. "Okay," she said, as if she had just made a decision, "you might as well know: the three of us, we're one of the Wednesday clubs. The Weird History Club."

The boys nodded.

Deciding these people *were* weird, I mumbled, "Sure," and flushed down my juice.

There was a silence until Jessica said, "It's sort of unusual for kids to start after the term begins. How'd you get in?"

I said, "I was told somebody dropped out."

"Right," Barney said, shooting a glance at Jessica—as if asking for her approval. "Austin."

"'Dropped out,'" said Mac, sneering. "They *would* tell you that."

Jessica said, "Bet no one told you *why* Austin"—she put up her fingers like quote marks—"'dropped out.'"

"Ms. Foxton said it was a sad story."

The kids exchanged looks as if sharing some secret. A bell rang.

"End of recess," Mac announced. They jumped up and hurried away.

I remained in my chair, thinking what an odd bunch they were. I even lifted my arm and sniffed, relieved not to smell anything bad.

Gulping down the rest of my muffin, I got up and found the steps. As if she had been waiting for me, Jessica appeared. "What do you think of our Weird History Club?" she asked as we started up.

Not wanting to say how uncomfortable they had made me feel, I muttered, "Okay."

We continued on without talking. When we reached the second floor, Jessica said, "You asked if bad things happened here. Well, that Austin kid, the one whose place you're taking, he disappeared."

I halted. *"Disappeared?* How'd that happen?"

"That's the purpose of the Weird History Club," she said. "You know, try to find out what the school hides."

Limping slightly, she veered away, but looked over her shoulder, smiled—she really had a great smile—and called, "Got to get a book. Welcome to the seventh year."

I finally checked my schedule. Every day was different. It was going to drive me nuts. At the moment I had math. I found the class. Once there I made an effort to follow the lesson—math—but couldn't and gave up. Instead, I kept thinking about Jessica's words: that the Penda School had happened because a kid died. I assumed she was talking about the boy in the painting, the one whose eyes were so full of fear. Or had someone else died?

As the morning went on with science class, I felt increasingly overwhelmed and uneasy. Penda was going to be hard. I also worried that I was not going to fit in. I suppose that made me automatically think of Uncle Charlie, because a moment later I saw him. It was as if thinking I was seeing him was my way of reassuring myself. *Yeah. It's good to see him here.*

Knowing I could call up his memory whenever I needed to, I felt my tension ease.

Lunch hour came after science class. The science teacher, who must have known I was new, suggested that two kids in my homeroom class, Peter and Sara, take me to lunch.

Sara said, "So, Tony, what do you think of the school so far?"

Not wanting to share my depressed thoughts, I said, "It's all right."

"It's good, really," said Peter.

Sara said, "A few losers, but most kids are nice."

Catching sight of that blond kid, I spun about. He was gone.

"Something the matter?" asked Peter.

Frustrated, I said, "There's this blond, curly-headed boy in our class. I keep seeing him, but he keeps . . . going away."

Puzzled, Peter turned to Sara. "Do you know who that is?"

Shaking her head, Sara gazed at me with curiosity. Her look was too much like the way Connecticut friends had reacted to Uncle Charlie's spooky talk. Not wanting to be labeled a weirdo again, I changed the subject. "Who are the losers?" I asked.

"Try the ones you sat next to in homeroom," said Sara, moving on. "Jessica and Mac. No one likes them."

"The Weird History Club," said Peter. "Total freaks."

"What do you mean?" I said.

"Dude," said Peter, "didn't you notice the black ties and neck scarves? Like, Penda has a dress code, but we're allowed *any* color tie or scarf. They have this Wednesday club, the Weird History Club. *Always* wear black."

Sara said, "Bet you anything they sat in class the way they did—an open seat between them—so you'd *have* to sit there."

"Why would they do that?"

"To get you to join their club," said Sara.

"Can't believe Batalie let them," said Peter. "Don't join."

"Right," added Sara. "They're the bad news on the late news."

Wanting to learn more about what Jessica had only hinted at, I said, "You guys know what happened to the kid I'm replacing? Somebody named Austin."

There was an awkward pause as Peter and Sara eyed each other.

Sara said, "Let's get lunch."

I couldn't miss it: *something* had happened to that Austin

kid, but other than the Weird History Club, people were not going to say. How come?

The cafeteria was much more crowded and louder than at recess. Everyone seemed to know everyone, but the only one I really knew was Uncle Charlie. That he appeared puzzled me, because I hadn't realized I had been thinking about him. Except I must have been, because when I told myself to stop thinking about him, he went.

I ate with Sara, Peter, and some other kids, trying to pay attention to the chatter. Not tuned in, I noticed Jessica, Mac, and Barney sitting at their table. At one point, Jessica looked up. Our eyes met. I turned away, not wanting to start at Penda linked to losers.

Peter leaned toward me. "See that kid over there?"

I was hoping he was going to point to the blond kid, but it was a tall, athletic boy sitting at the middle of a table, surrounded by other kids all having a loud time.

"What about him?"

"Riley Fadden," said Peter. "Eights. Student Council president. Great basketball player. Ditto lacrosse. Academic Honors Award. School loves him. The perfect Penda student. With him as your role model, you can't go wrong."

"Thanks," I said, discouraged because I wasn't that way

and never would be. All the same, I thought of that time Uncle Charlie had called me perfect. I never had asked him what he meant.

The ground shook. Dishes rattled for a few seconds. "What's *that*?" I cried, automatically grabbing the edge of the table.

Peter shrugged with indifference. "Earthquake. Oh, right, you come from back east. California has thousands of earthquakes each year."

"*Thousands?*"

"Nothing to worry about." He grinned, amused at my discomfort. "Unless it's the big one."

"What's 'the big one'?"

"The major earthquake they say is going to happen here someday."

"Which means . . . ?"

"The school collapses and we all die." Peter laughed.

The thought I'd had before returned: *There's a lot of death attached to this school.*

The day was long, but I got through. At Penda, at three o'clock you were supposed to check in at homeroom before leaving. But when I did, Batalie asked me if I would mind staying after school, saying, "We should go over some things."

Knowing I was heading home to an empty apartment, I said, "Sure."

"Have you picked a sport?" he began.

I shook my head.

"You'll need to. Along with a Wednesday club."

Jessica must have overheard the remark, because as she left the room, she looked at me and smiled. I was flattered by her interest.

"I'll be right back," said Mr. Batalie. "I want to get things you'll need. Take a look at the class portraits. Good way to know people." He left the room. In the hallway I saw him chat briefly with Jessica and then walk off.

I was alone—except for Uncle Charlie, who was looking at me from the back of the room. "Was this place as creepy when you were here?" I called to him.

When he faded away, I muttered, "Thanks."

I stood by the picture wall, which had a headshot of every student in the class. Under the pictures there was a banner, which read:

ONLY SIGNED <u>POSITIVE</u> REMARKS
ALLOWED.
NO NEGATIVITY.

Beneath each picture was a sheet of paper on which people had scrawled comments.

Great response paper. Rich
Loved your polka-dot neck scarf. Lucy
Terrific soccer player. Mia

There were many messages for some people. I guessed they were the popular kids. Others had fewer. Under Mac's picture, one remark: *Your ideas are curious. Jessica*

Under Jessica's picture, it read: *The way you look at things is cool. Mac.*

A second line: *You have original ideas. Mac.*

I got it: The Weird History Club people kept to themselves, or were forced to. "The freaks," as Peter had said.

I checked for a picture of that blond, curly-headed boy, the one I kept seeing, or thought I kept seeing. I didn't find him, but there was that blank space. Was it Austin's? The kid who disappeared? Was it going to be mine? Sort of strange to think I was going to take a disappeared kid's place.

Batalie returned, papers in hand. Noticing where I was standing, he said, "I change the comment-board sheets every week. Please note: only signed, positive remarks.

Anonymous, negative stuff is forbidden."

"Is there a picture of everyone?" I asked.

"Absolutely. Right, I'll need to put your picture up. Let's take one." He set the papers on his desk, pulled out a phone, and aimed it at me. "Smile."

"I don't, much."

"Well, starting a new school in a new town is hard. And someone close to you died. So sorry."

How, I asked myself, *do all these people know about Uncle Charlie?*

I said, "There's one kid's picture I don't see."

"Who's that?"

"I don't know his name. Blond, curly-haired boy."

Batalie looked up sharply, alarm in his eyes.

"You know," I said. "The kid who looks like the painting in the school office."

"Oh, the Penda Boy." Batalie forced a laugh. "We like to say his *spirit* is *in* Penda, but not in class."

I was about to reply, *But I keep seeing him*, but checked myself, since I wasn't really sure I *had* seen him. Instead, I said, "Mr. Batalie, I'm replacing someone named Austin, right?"

The alarm in Batalie's eyes intensified.

I said, "What . . . what happened to him?"

Batalie turned to his desk. "Let's go over some things. Have a computer?"

"Uh-huh."

"Good. The school posts daily notices. Homework. School closings." He began to give me papers. "English assignments for the term. Honesty code. School rules. The usual. Ask Mrs. Z for a list of this term's teams."

I was sure he was racing through things to get me out of there because of my questions.

"Play basketball?" he said.

I shook my head.

"Too bad. I could use your height," he said. "Field-trip dates. List of supplies for class. School calendar, including holidays. School phone numbers to keep at home. Student directory from the opening of the term, with addresses, email, and phone numbers. Changes made online. Your info will be sent out by the end of the week."

I stuffed everything into my backpack.

Batalie held out his hand. We shook. "Tony, so glad you've joined us. Your picture will be on the wall soon." He smiled. "That'll make you official." He was telling me to leave.

I moved toward the door only to halt. "Can I ask one more question?"

"Of course."

"How come no one wants to say what happened to that Austin kid?"

Batalie took off his glasses, breathed on them, and cleaned them with a small black cloth. Only then did he look up, fear back in his eyes.

What he said, however, was, "Let's just say we've all agreed not to talk about it. Tony," he went on briskly, "you've had a great start. Don't worry about assignments these first few days. Give yourself some time. Have a good night." He shifted away, ending our talk.

I went into the hallway. It was deserted, and a deserted school is the emptiest place in the world. *What*, I asked myself, *happened to Austin? How come no one wants to talk about him?* The way Batalie had reacted to my questions about Austin and the blond kid made me think they were connected—somehow. Since I was taking Austin's spot, it made me uneasy.

I walked down the hall, my feet silent on the carpeted floor. At the top of the big steps, I looked down. The blond boy was at the bottom, as if waiting for me. "Hey," I called out.

Some man—he looked like a teacher—stepped out of the school office right in front of the kid. The teacher turned toward me. "Were you calling me?" he said.

"No, sir."

"Well, have a good night." He smiled, waved, and walked off. The blond kid had vanished.

I stood where I was. The teacher had acted as if he hadn't seen the boy.

I had.

But it had all been so quick, I had to ask myself, "Did I?"

When I reached the street, students had gone. Other than a few shallow puddles, no trace of the morning's storm remained. The air was fresh. Above, the sky was clear save for some high-flying birds silhouetted against white clouds, their wings flapping slowly, like shadows waving good-bye. Cars and trucks rattled by. People passed, going about their business. No one noticed me. New kid. New city. New school.

Suddenly exhausted, I stripped off Dad's tie and stuffed it into my backpack. As I stood there, thinking through the day, I looked back at the school. I thought—as I had before— that there couldn't be many school buildings like it: old and quirky, with all those roofs and towers, the outside sort of like a twisted Rubik's Cube, the inside like a funeral home.

My eyes went to the tallest tower, and I remembered what Ms. Foxton had said: that no one was allowed in the towers. But I *had* seen someone up there. Or thought so.

I turned for home only to have the feeling that I was being

watched. I spun about. Seeing no one, I shifted my gaze back to the high tower. A face appeared behind the highest tower window. I stared. He looked like that blond boy. Next moment he disappeared.

That's when I had a new thought: the face in the tower when my parents and I had first looked at the school, the boy in the school office painting, and the kid I kept seeing around the school—it seemed crazy, but they all seemed like the same person.

I had heard enough ghost talk from Uncle Charlie to make me think that whoever the kid was—here one moment, gone the next—he (or it) was acting like a ghost. Trouble was, I didn't believe in ghosts. After all, that supernatural talk from Uncle Charlie had just been that, talk—his way of acting like a kid.

Ghosts don't exist, I told myself. *It's all a joke. Don't be stupid. Maybe this was what Ms. Foxton had warned me about: I was being teased.*

But who would be teasing me?

I used my key to let myself into our apartment, dropped my backpack by the door, and plopped on our old sofa, which we had brought from back east. When I sat, the pillows seemed to sigh, reminding me of Uncle Charlie's last breath. There I was, sitting in an empty apartment, the walls white and blank, the inside of nothing. It didn't even smell like home, just paint. I thought, *This newness is getting old*.

How different from Connecticut. When I came home from school, Uncle Charlie would be there. We'd talk, do things, have fun.

Next moment Uncle Charlie, like the genie from a lamp, was standing across the room.

"What's going on?" I asked him.

He smiled and vanished.

I asked myself: *What makes Uncle Charlie appear the way he does?* I mean, just now, I *had* been thinking of him. Then, *abracadabra*—I saw him. Okay. *Memory*. Even so, there'd been a number of times that day I had *not* been thinking of him, and still he had appeared.

I told myself that having his memory around had gotten me through the first day. *Fine. Time to move on*. I would only think about him—and bring him around—when *I* felt the need.

I pulled out the assignment sheets teachers had given me. End of October, a five-page research paper for history. Mid-November, an English paper. Before Christmas break, a science lab report. Heart sinking, I threw the assignment list aside. I had never been asked to write a paper before.

I took a long shower. Thinking again about what Jessica had said, that I smelled like death, I scrubbed myself hard.

I went to my room and walked my slackline. When I did, I felt free. Uncle Charlie had told me that walking the line was not of the earth, not of the sky, but what a ghost might feel. How, I asked myself, had he come up with that idea?

Sometimes when I walked the line, I didn't think of anything other than what I was doing. If I didn't concentrate, I fell. In fact, when I heard the apartment door slam, I did fall.

Dad looked into my room. "How come you're on the floor?"

"I stopped being a ghost."

"Very funny. Do you like Penda?"

"It's fine. How come you're home early?"

"It's your first day. Didn't want you to be here alone."

"I'm good."

"Okay," Dad said, retreating.

The trouble with most parents is that they believe what their kids tell them.

I got back on the slackline but kept falling. In a corner, Uncle Charlie reappeared. He was becoming like one of those songs you really love. You know, the kind you can't get out of your head until, though you love it, it starts becoming annoying.

Since I was convinced I had *not* been thinking about him, that question my cousins and I had always asked popped into my head: *What's the deal with Uncle Charlie?*

Telling myself I was being unfair, I changed the question to: *What's the deal with the school?*

Mom opened my door and held up some white foam boxes. "San Francisco has amazing food!" she exclaimed.

I said, "Hope you got McDonald's."

"Very funny. Chinese. *Northern* Chinese, thank you. Dinner's ready."

At the table she said, "How was school?"

"Okay."

"Make any friends?"

"Maybe."

"Need anything?"

"Pens, pencils, notebooks."

Mom said, "Can we wait for the weekend?"

"Suppose."

To Dad, I said, "What do you know about earthquakes here?"

"California has about ten thousand earthquakes a year.

Most are small. Maybe a few hundred are greater than 3.0 magnitude. Only about fifteen to twenty are greater than 4.0."

"How do you *know* that?"

"The US government has a website that lists the day's earthquakes. San Francisco is famous for them."

"Hey, did you guys tell the school about Uncle Charlie and me?"

Mom, shaking her head, looked at Dad.

Dad said, "I didn't. They don't need to know."

"They *do* know."

Dad shrugged. "If you told them, that's okay."

But I hadn't.

Later, in bed, as I was trying to sleep, an idea came: Uncle Charlie must have told Penda I was coming to the school.

Only I realized that was impossible: I had been accepted at Penda *after* he died. But *someone* must have told them about Uncle Charlie. If it wasn't my parents, or me, then who?

I started thinking about that boy I kept seeing around the school and in the tower: how he looked like the kid in the school office painting, the one they called the Penda Boy.

Not possible, I told myself again.

I felt an urge to get to school and look at that painting once more. I was certain that it would *not* be the kid I kept seeing, for the simple reason that that was impossible.

The first thing I did when I woke the next morning was look around for Uncle Charlie. He was not there. Good. That told me I could handle my memories. One problem solved.

Next, when I got to school, I went right into the school office. Mrs. Z, sitting behind her desk, looked up. "Hello, Tony. How did your first day go?"

"Fine. I'm supposed to ask you for a list of the sports teams I can join."

"Good idea."

As she bent over to get the list from a drawer, I looked at the painting of the Penda Boy. My heart sank. The kid in the painting really did look like the boy I kept seeing.

Mrs. Z handed me a sheet of paper.

"Mrs. Z," I said, pointing to the painting. "He died, right?"

"The Penda Boy? Oh yes, a long time ago. In the high tower, they say."

I left and headed up the steps, my thoughts on the Penda Boy. *When impossible things happen, does that make them possible?* I looked around to the other steps. I didn't see the boy, only Uncle Charlie.

Exasperated, I told myself that whenever I felt upset, Uncle

Charlie appeared, as if I was asking him for help.

"I don't need you," I called out.

"You talking to me?" said some kid right behind me.

"No, sorry," I said, and hurried on, trying not to think of the boy.

As I went from class to class, I felt I was being judged by students and teachers. In various subjects—science, art, and math—teachers kept asking if I had learned this or that, as if constantly saying, *Do you know anything?* Not much, apparently. And there were kids who asked, "Who are you?" That made me feel more isolated than ever.

No sooner did I feel alone than Uncle Charlie appeared. I told him—in my head—*Uncle Charlie, I'm trying to get along without you.* That seemed to satisfy him. He went.

But not the blond boy. I kept seeing him, always partly veiled by a crowd of kids. I tried a new tactic: When I saw him, I closed my eyes for a few seconds. When I opened them, he was gone. That convinced me: I could switch him off the way I did my memory of Uncle Charlie.

And, following my decision not to hang with losers, I also avoided Jessica and her friends. I was never going to be with the *in* group, but once you are with the losers, you're a loser forever.

The next day, my face appeared on the homeroom portrait wall. I *had* taken Austin's place. Below my picture, things were already written.

Welcome to Penda! Mr. Batalie
You're very interesting. Jessica
I'm glad you're in our class. Lilly
I need to talk to you.

Why did Jessica find me interesting? Who was Lilly? Who needed to talk to me? Weren't all comments supposed to be signed?

Sure enough, the following day, Thursday, just before classes began, Mr. Batalie made an announcement. "Okay, guys, someone wrote under Tony's picture. Nothing negative, but it was *not* signed. I trust we all know the rules about the portrait board. *No unsigned statements.* I've removed that comment. Whoever did that, please do not do it again."

Kids looked around. No one confessed. Nothing more was said. Or answered.

Later in the day, Peter asked me if I would like to sit on the newspaper Wednesday club. I agreed, only to have Jessica ask me to join the Weird History Club. She said, "I need to talk to you."

"I promised Peter," I said, but noted that *I need to talk to you* was what had been written under my photo. Had she written it?

I sat in on the School Newspaper Club. They talked about who should interview the *perfect* Riley Fadden. It made me wish I had gone with Jessica.

Thursday crept by like a slug with a flat tire. I did not see Uncle Charlie, and that was good. But the blond kid kept appearing, which I did not like. Whenever I saw him, I turned and moved on. That helped.

The best part of my day was after school, when I walked the slackline. Though I was getting better and better, school was not. I felt stupid in classes. I was not making any friends and wasn't sure how to do anything about it.

Friday, another comment appeared under my picture: *I need to talk to you.* Once more, it wasn't signed. By then I was sure it was Jessica who had written it, but I didn't want to say anything.

Batalie scolded the class. No one admitted doing anything.

I saw the blond boy twice.

The instant I saw him, not only did I turn away, but I hung around other kids. That seemed to work. He went. From then on, I made sure to stay around people.

All the same, I kept catching glimpses of him. So I changed my mind about Jessica. The way I kept seeing—or *thinking* I was seeing—the blond kid upset me. Jessica claimed her club studied weird things. Seeing the Penda Boy was totally weird. I was also sure she wanted to talk to me. Maybe she would help get the boy out of my head. This was why, during morning recess, in the cafeteria, I headed right to where she and the Weird History Club were sitting.

Jessica was at her table, one of her feet—black sneakers with red shoelaces—on the empty chair. When I showed up, doughnut and juice in hand, I didn't get her regular smile. It took me looking at her foot to get her to move so I could sit.

"How's it going?" I said.

"We're okay," she replied, sounding glum. Mac and Barney kept eating and didn't speak. It was as if they knew I had been avoiding them.

After some silence, Mac said, "Hey, Tony, what do you think of the Penda School now?"

I said, "A lot of work."

"Yeah," agreed Barney, adding to his sunflower-seed pile. "It is."

I was trying to get up my nerve to ask Jessica about the blond kid when she suddenly said, "Anyone tell you more about Austin?"

I shook my head.

"They won't," she said.

"Why?" I asked.

Mac left off biting a fingernail to say, "The towers. Learn about them yet?"

"Not really," I said, not getting what Austin had to do with the towers.

"They're haunted," Mac said, going back to chewing his nail.

Remembering Ms. Foxton's warning about the teasing of new students with haunted stories, I said, "Yeah, right." Same time I wondered why only these kids were teasing me.

"No," said Barney. "It's true."

"That's why they don't let anyone inside them," said Mac.

"They *say* it's for safety reasons," added Barney.

"Actually," said Mac, "she doesn't want us to see what's up there."

"Who's *she*?" I asked.

Jessica said, "Ms. Foxton."

"She's afraid of what we'll find," Mac said.

"The ghost," I said.

Jessica said, "Yeah, the ghost."

I couldn't hold back. "What if I told you that the first time I was here, I saw a kid at one of the tower windows?"

The boys' mouths dropped open. Jessica sat up straight, eyes right on me. "Who'd you see?" she demanded. "We need to know."

Glad to get some reaction, I said, "When my parents and I first visited the school—Sunday—at the highest tower's window—I saw a boy looking out."

Jessica said, "That true?"

"I think so."

The boys looked at Jessica as if she should reply. After studying me for a bit, she said, "Then you saw the ghost."

"What . . . ghost?"

She said, "The Penda Boy."

"The kid whose picture is in the school office?" I asked.

"Yeah," said Mac.

I waited a second before saying, "Has anyone else seen him?"

No one spoke until Jessica said, "You were close to someone who died, right? Bet you anything the Penda Boy thinks—because of your smell—that you're dead enough to be his friend. But I hate to tell you, he's not your friend—he's an enemy."

"You serious?" I cried as the bell went off for the end of recess.

"Hey," said Jessica, standing up. "You're the one who told us you saw him. No one else is seeing the ghost. Want to know how to handle him? Join our club."

Defensively, I said, "Please don't write any more comments under my picture."

"Wasn't me," she said, and the three went off.

Shaken, I sat there thinking: *It can't be a ghost. I don't want anything to do with ghosts.* I shut my eyes. When I opened them, Uncle Charlie was sitting opposite me.

Frustrated, I said to him, as firmly as I could, "Okay. From here on, I am *not* going to remember you. Get it? I'm on my own."

He went.

I headed for class, not sure what I felt more: angry, annoyed, or just creeped out.

Right before lunch, Batalie called me up to his desk. "Ms. Foxton asked that you stop in her office during fifth period. You can be late for science." He handed me a late slip.

My mind still churning over what Jessica had said, I felt lousy and had no desire to see Ms. Foxton. Not having a choice, I went.

Mrs. Z greeted me. "Ms. Foxton will be with you in a minute."

I sat down on the office couch and stared at the painting of the Penda Boy. Absolutely, he was the kid I kept seeing. My big question kept coming back: If he was a ghost—as Jessica said—how come I was the only one seeing him?

"Ms. Foxton is free now," said Mrs. Z.

As I entered her office, Ms. Foxton stood up behind her desk. "Tony," she said, "so glad to see you again. Please, have a seat."

She sat, clasped her small, well-manicured hands, and smiled. "How are things going?" she asked.

Preoccupied by thoughts of the Penda Boy, I just sat there.

"Getting on with Mr. Batalie?" she prompted. "The other teachers?"

"I think so."

She waited a moment, then said, "Have any impressions to share?"

"Not really."

"Any problems?"

"Nope," I said. For a second I thought of telling her about the Penda Boy. Not wanting her to think I was nutty, I didn't.

"Do you think you'll be happy here?"

"I suppose," I said mechanically, wanting only to leave.

She frowned. My blank responses were frustrating her. I was hoping she would dismiss me, but she said, "I know that developing friendships is one of the most important things one can do at a new school. In addition, you're also new to the city. Have you had the chance to make friends?"

She waited for me to speak, so I felt I had to say something. What popped out was the first name that came into my head. "Well, Jessica, sort of."

"Jessica Richards?"

Hearing alarm in her voice, I was sorry I had spoken. Besides, I was not sure I wanted Jessica to be my friend.

Ms. Foxton gazed at me, fright back in her eyes. "Tony," she said with care, "one's choice of friends is always important in one's school life. No doubt, Jessica has her . . . good points. I'm just not certain," she went on, her voice dropping almost to a whisper, "that she's your best choice for a friend."

"What's wrong with her?" I said, not believing she was actually telling me who I should be friends with.

"Jessica has been known to . . . create . . . problems."

"What . . . what kind of problems?"

"Well . . ."

I made my own connection. "You talking about the Weird History Club?"

The fear in Ms. Foxton's eyes deepened. "Ah," she said,

"you know about . . . them."

"Uh-huh."

"Do you . . . intend to join?"

Having no idea what I'd do, I shrugged.

"What has Jessica told you?"

Not wanting to talk about ghosts, I said, "The kid I replaced—that Austin kid—the club is trying to find out what happened to him."

Ms. Foxton's hands gripped together so tightly the tips of her fingers turned white. "Tony," she said, her voice low with tension, "let's just say that Jessica has a reputation for creating difficulties. For instance, telling . . . fanciful stories. I'm afraid . . . truthfulness is not one of her better character traits."

She *was* telling me who my friends should be.

This time Ms. Foxton actually whispered. "Tony, I need to be as direct as I can: We want you to be happy here. But we also need to know you can be a positive member of the Penda family. What you choose to do with your . . . friendships is a big part of education and . . . your life."

Upset, I just sat there. As if coming to my rescue, Uncle Charlie stood behind her.

Ms. Foxton gazed at me for a while and then said, "The great Greek philosopher Aristotle said, 'A friend is one soul in two bodies.' When choosing a friend, you might ask yourself: Do you wish to share souls with that person?"

Uncle Charlie grinned.

"I'll think about it," I said, not sure what she was getting at. Besides, I was angry.

"Please understand," she went on, "my responsibility is the well-being of Penda."

"Right. Respect the past—protect the future."

She paled and suddenly stood. "Thank you for coming, Tony."

Dismissed, I hauled myself up and hurried toward the door.

"Tony," Ms. Foxton called—I heard apology in her voice— "if you can think of any way I can be helpful, my door is always open. I mean that, sincerely."

I walked out, ignoring how Mrs. Z looked at me—as if she had overheard and disapproved of the conversation.

I headed up one of the big stairways toward science class. All I could think was: *Why was Ms. Foxton warning me about Jessica? What is she worried about? Why is everyone so evasive about Austin?*

I looked across to the other steps. The Penda Boy was there, his eyes full of pleading, as if desperate to say something to me.

Feeling a bolt of anger, I called, "What do you want from me?"

A student came bounding down the steps.

The Penda Boy vanished.

I stood there, trying to make sense of it all. I couldn't. All I had was what Jessica had said: the boy I kept seeing was not just a ghost. He was my enemy.

For the rest of the day I made sure not to be alone.

At three o'clock, I couldn't get out of school fast enough. On the sidewalk, kids were milling around, sorting out plans for the weekend. Having no plans, I felt like a weed in a fancy garden. I looked around for Jessica, wanting to talk to her some more. Not seeing her, I figured she had gone home. But to my exasperation, I saw Uncle Charlie. I swung away only to see a kid come right toward me.

"Tony?" he said.

It took a second for me to realize it was the kid who had been pointed out to me as "the perfect Penda student."

"We haven't met," he said, holding out his hand like a professional greeter. "I'm Riley Fadden, Eights Student Council president. You've probably heard of me. Glad to welcome you to Penda."

"Thanks."

"Problems with the school, whatever, come to me. I'm Mr. Fix-It. Or there's a council rep in the Sevens. Peter Schotter. You can always talk to him."

"Okay."

He edged closer. "Give you a tip," he said, as if I was some special friend. "Keep away from that Weird History Club. I mean, that Jessica"—he grinned—"she's awesome pretty, but"—he punched me lightly on my shoulder—"honest. She's trouble."

He walked away, calling, "Have a great weekend."

That did it. They were all worried about Jessica because she was trying to find out school secrets. Okay, I had to know a lot of things:

First, that old question: What's the deal with Uncle Charlie? Why did he keep coming into my head? He was like an assigned guide—nice when you first get to a new place, but then you want to be on your own. I reminded myself that he was just a memory. Memories can fade.

He was different from the Penda Boy, right? But that gave me the second question: Was I really seeing the Penda Boy's ghost, or just imagining him?

Third, if the boy *was* a ghost, how come *I* was the only one seeing him?

As far as I could tell, the only ones who could give me

answers were the Weird History Club. The school losers.

So, fourth question: Should I have anything to do with them?

At dinner that night, my parents tried to get me to talk about school. "Pick a sport?" Dad asked.

"Think it will be Ping-Pong," I said.

Dad said, "That's sure to get you an athletic scholarship to Stanford."

"That's why I chose it."

"Tell us about your new friends," said Mom.

"Ms. Foxton warned me about having the wrong ones."

"Who did she mean?"

I shrugged.

Mom looked at Dad, then back at me. "Is this going to be a problem?" she asked.

"I'm good."

Back in my room, I snatched up the school student directory, flipped to the seventh-grade listings, and found Jessica's name, address, and phone number.

I called. "It's Tony, the new kid."

"You going to join us?" was the first thing she said.

Avoiding the question, I said, "That kid, Austin, the one I'm replacing—how come no one wants to say what happened to him?"

She said, "Guess how many kids have disappeared from the Penda School over the years."

"Disappeared? What are you talking about?"

"Like, twelve."

"You serious?"

"That's the whole point. The school doesn't want anyone to know. The Weird History Club tries to find out the truth. If you join us, you could help us find out."

I said, "Ms. Foxton warned me about becoming your friend."

"Idiot. Bet she won't last long in the school. Heads never do."

"Riley Fadden warned me about you too."

"Total jerk. Anyway, let me know if you want to join. You'd be great."

Flattered but uneasy, I didn't know what to say.

"You don't like to hear it," she went on, "but there's something dead about you, okay? Just be careful."

"Careful?"

"I read somewhere that the way people smell has a lot to do with relationships. If a ghost wanted you for a friend, you smelling like death might be a good place to start, right?"

"I thought you said he was my enemy."

"Hey, enemies start off pretending to be best friends.

Right? You keep asking about Austin. Okay: the ghost in the tower—the one you saw—we're pretty sure he's the one that caused Austin and all those others to disappear."

Abruptly, she hung up.

I sat there thinking, *The ghost—if he is a ghost—is not going to be my friend. I don't want to disappear like Austin. And I don't want to see Uncle Charlie again. I want to be on my own.*

I walked my slackline. I went forward. I went back. I didn't fall. Then I went into the living room, where my parents were working.

I said, "Forgot to tell you I need more things for school."

Dad, still working his tablet, said, "Like what?"

"I need more ties. Including a black one."

"A black one?" said Mom. "For goodness sake, why?"

"It's the insignia for a club I'm thinking of joining."

"What club?" Dad asked.

"A history club, sort of."

Dad looked around. "Why black?"

"History is about dead people, isn't it?"

I walked the slackline for a long time. It was a relief to think of nothing.

That weekend, my family worked on the apartment, throwing out old stuff, making lists of what we needed, buying new things (including school things), putting pictures on the walls, books on shelves. All Saturday I couldn't stop thinking about Jessica, the Weird History Club, and the blond kid I kept seeing, the Penda Boy, the ghost.

By Sunday morning, it was as if I had made a turn on the slackline, moving in a new direction, a direction *away* from Jessica and her club. I knew why too—those warnings, Ms. Foxton's, Riley Fadden's, plus the things other kids said: keep away from Jessica. She was forceful. She made trouble. But mostly it was what she'd said to me, that the ghost was after me in some way, trying to make me disappear, like that Austin kid. I kept telling myself it wasn't true, and I didn't want to hear it.

I considered bringing up my memory of Uncle Charlie. Maybe he could help me. Then I told myself I needed to handle things on my own. As far as I was concerned, it was time to forget him. If I could ease him away, I could do the same with that so-called ghost.

That was why, over the next week, I just went from class to class, avoiding Jessica and the club. Same time, I tried to be with people. Tried out the science Wednesday club. Not interesting. But just doing new things seemed to work. I didn't see Uncle Charlie. Good. I was managing him. Though I did see that blond kid, it was only a few times. I was more convinced than ever that it *was* just me. I was upset with Uncle Charlie's death, the new city, and the new school. Things seemed to be getting better.

Then Friday came.

It was three o'clock. School was over. Kids gathered on the street. I hung around as people made plans to get together or told one another what they were going to do that weekend. Since the only plans I had were with my parents, I was hoping someone would invite me to do something. All of a sudden, I remembered I had left my backpack in class.

I tore up the steps and into room seven, my homeroom. Soon as I got there, I saw the blond boy sitting where I had been sitting. My backpack was in his lap, and it looked like he was putting something into it.

"Hey!" I shouted. "Don't touch that!"

Next second Mr. Batalie walked in.

When he did, the boy vanished, and my backpack fell to the floor.

"Did you forget something?" asked Mr. Batalie.

"Backpack," I managed to say.

"Have a nice weekend," he called as I ran out.

I got into the hallway and opened my bag. On top of my school junk was a piece of paper on which was scrawled

Please talk to me.

I was unable to deny what was going on: I was being stalked by a ghost.

I rushed back down to the street, determined to ask the first kid from my class I saw if they wanted to do something together that weekend. But when I reached the sidewalk, everyone was gone.

By the time I got home, I knew I absolutely had to talk to Jessica. She seemed to be the only person who could give me advice about the ghost. I could have called her right then, but I decided it would be better to speak in person. I wanted— needed—to see her reaction.

On Monday, I'd tell her everything.

Over the weekend, my parents and I did what Mom kept urging us to do: take in the sights of San Francisco.

Saturday, a sunny day, we rode a cable car, took a boat ride around the bay, visited Alcatraz, walked across the Golden Gate Bridge, and ate at a Chinese restaurant. As we strolled about, we passed a men's clothing store with ties in the windows. I got my folks to get me a black one.

Sunday, after sleeping in, I did homework. In the afternoon, we went to Golden Gate Park and the Legion of Honor art museum.

"I love being in this city," exclaimed Mom as we returned to our apartment after a Brazilian dinner. "Don't you think it's full of life?" she asked.

That was what Uncle Charlie had said about the Penda School. All I said was, "It's okay."

"Sourpuss," said Mom, smiling.

Sunday night I walked my slackline but kept falling. I knew the answer too. I was worried about the Penda Boy.

At about nine, my cell phone rang. It was the first time that had happened since I moved to San Francisco.

It was Jessica. "Hey, you going to join the club or not?"

"I was going to talk to you tomorrow."

"You know where to find me." She hung up.

I lay on my bed, thinking: *Jessica wants me to be part of the club. She said the club tries to find out school secrets. I want answers about the ghost. About Austin.*

I wanted friends too. Did I want her as a friend? I had been cautioned about her. By who? Riley Fadden. Ms. Foxton. People I didn't like. Okay. I'd be friends with Jessica. Join the Weird History Club. Hopefully, she would help me decide what to do about the ghost. I had to get him out of my head, the same way I had gotten rid of Uncle Charlie.

When I woke Monday morning, it was dark outside. For a moment, I thought I had gotten up too early. Then I realized: it was the famous San Francisco fog.

During breakfast, Mom said, "Remember how Uncle Charlie liked to recite that poem, 'The fog comes on little cat feet. It sits looking over harbor and city on silent haunches and then moves on.' No idea who he was quoting."

"Carl Sandburg," said Dad. "Writing about Chicago."

I shook my head clear. Having Uncle Charlie in my head would *not* help. This was the day I was going to talk to Jessica about the ghost.

Together, my parents and I stepped out of the apartment into thick, swirling fog. What sounded like heavy groaning filled the air. "What's that?" I asked.

Dad said, "It's the angel Gabriel atop your school announcing the end of the world." In a mock low voice he added, "The dead will soon rise."

I stared at him.

"Don't be morbid," snapped Mom. To me, she said, "Just foghorns from the bay." She peered into my already damp face. "Can you get to school okay?"

"It's only six blocks."

They moved away, Mom calling, "Have a great day. Love you."

I watched them dissolve into the fog. Then I turned toward school, only to be engulfed by the dense mist.

Unable to see beyond a foot or two, I walked with care, my feet making soft pit-pats on the sidewalk. Foghorns moaned. The swirling fog played hide-and-seek with the world. The air smelled wet. I was wet. Buildings rose up into nothingness, while solid things became oddly shaped. Red and green traffic lights were bleary, blinking eyes. Car headlights were uncertain flashlights, and on the damp roads, tires hissed like spitting snakes. From somewhere came a screeching siren, which I assumed was an ambulance. The drifting gray shadows that crept by were like people in a fake horror movie. I felt clammy, uncomfortable, confused, as if I were walking through an ever-changing maze.

Muddled, I stopped and tried to figure out where I was. I couldn't. I took out my cell phone to check the time. It was dead. I had forgotten to charge it. When I peered back to see where I had started, I couldn't.

I turned around, only to become more jumbled, hesitant about which way to go. Uncle Charlie's words, "The separation between past, present, and future is only an illusion," filled my head. It felt that way. Not wanting to go the wrong way, I stood still.

Without warning, an old man loomed out of the fog and

peered so closely into my face that I saw his lively eyes. As if he knew I was lost, he grabbed hold of my arm and shoved me forcibly a few steps until I saw a street sign I recognized. I knew where I was. "Thanks," I muttered as the old man disappeared into the fog.

It took two seconds for me to realize that the man who had helped me was Uncle Charlie.

Except he had not *just* helped me: he had taken *hold* of my arm and guided me to safety. I spun about and gazed into the murk where he had vanished. "Uncle Charlie!" I called. "Uncle Charlie!"

I had *felt* his touch. Except . . . that was impossible. He was dead. He was a memory.

Heart hammering, struggling to catch my breath, I considered going back to the apartment, staying home from school. I reached for my phone only to remember it was dead. Like Uncle Charlie. Anyway, how could I explain not going to school? My parents would think I was insane.

Maybe I was.

Almost falling, I stumbled off a curb onto the street, only to have a huge black hearse leap out of the fog from behind a steep hill, like a black fish breaching from the sea. I jumped back. Unnerved, I looked all ways before I started across the street again. A kid ran past me. He looked like the Penda Boy.

Mid-street, I froze. What was happening?

A car horn blared at me. Startled, I bolted for the far curb, wanting to be with people. Forcing myself to go on, I kept searching my mind back to what had happened, or what I thought had happened: that Uncle Charlie had *touched* me.

I reached the school, where, if anything, the fog was denser. Kids drifted about, coming, going, solid one moment, dissolving the next. I couldn't tell who was who. I looked up. The school towers were wrapped in drifting gray. Same for that tall tree. The school seemed only partly there, the way I felt.

I moved toward the entryway, wanting to get inside. As I started up the steps, I saw the Penda Boy peering out from behind the doors, waiting for me.

I whirled about and stood in place, heart pounding, desperate to know what he wanted from me. The question fused with my fright about the old man I had seen, the one who had touched me, helped me. Because if it had been Uncle Charlie, and he was just a memory, how could he have *touched* me? I could make no sense of it—or him—or me.

"Tony."

Taken by surprise, I turned.

Standing close was a girl wearing a yellow slicker and a lavender scarf around her neck. Her face was wet, her smile big. Though she was familiar, I was so upset that I couldn't recall her name.

"Hi," she said, her smile turning tentative as she searched for recognition in my eyes. "Lilly," she said. "Your class? I didn't mean to startle you. Don't you love the fog?"

I remembered. "Oh, sure. Lilly."

"Right," said the girl, head cocked to one side in self-mockery. "Just me. Anyway, it's my birthday this week. Oh my God, thirteen." She lifted her shoulders as if squeezed by the huge event. "So, I'm having a party. Friday. Bunch of kids from class. Movie, go for pizza. Don't have to bring a present. Can you come?"

"Think so," I said, recovering. "Thanks. Thirteen, congrats."

"Give you info later," she said, and darted away as if she had acted boldly and needed the protection of three giggling girls who were watching.

Belatedly, I realized that Lilly had to be the girl who'd written the comment that she was glad I was in the class. I was annoyed. I was embarrassed. I was pleased. Mostly I was tense, sensing that unclear things were swirling around me—the fog, the Penda Boy, Uncle Charlie. Even Lilly.

Telling myself, *Calm down. There must be reasons*, I checked the doors. No longer seeing the Penda Boy, I went into school.

When I reached homeroom, I took an isolated desk. Breathing deeply, I tried to settle myself and make sense of what had happened by looking out the window at the heavy fog. *It's all in my head*, I kept telling myself. *It's all in my head.* Except I no longer knew what or who was in my head.

After a while, I stole a look over to where Lilly was sitting. She must have sensed my glance, because she peeked over her shoulder and smiled shyly at me. I forced a return smile. Then I caught Jessica watching me, a reminder that I had promised to speak to her. With so much tumbling in my head, I couldn't. Instead, I tried to pay attention to Batalie, who, thankfully, called the class to order.

I acted as if I was there. The truth is I didn't know where I was.

An hour and an half later, the recess bell rang. As students rushed out, I realized Jessica had stayed at her desk reading a textbook. I was sure she was waiting for me. Though too tense to talk, I made myself go up to her.

"Hey, Tony. What's up?"

"I sort of want to talk about . . . you know."

"Sure. Come on."

"How about Wednesday, after school?"

She focused her dark eyes on me and pushed back her hair. "Don't want to be seen with me?"

"I want more time."

For a moment, her eyes were fierce, like those in that painting of Mrs. Penda. "Okay," she said. "Let me know." She went off, flipping a forgiving smile over her shoulder.

During recess, I stayed at my desk thinking about Uncle Charlie, endlessly replaying what had happened when I came to school in the fog. Had Uncle Charlie been there or not? If yes, what *was* he? I thought of the expression *touched by memories*. Yeah, but not *really* touched.

I gazed out the windows. There was as much fog inside my mind as there was outside. I was asking myself, *If you are crazy, do you know you are crazy?*

Seventh-grade history was a European survey, from the fall of the Roman Empire to the eighteenth century. We were up to medieval times. The teacher, Mr. Bokor, was an enormous guy from Haiti, big enough to be an NFL linebacker except he wore baggy brown suits. He had a deep, lilting voice, which filled the classroom. As he moved among students, he was always dramatic, often funny, poking kids' shoulders to make a point or to hold their attention. He had the kind of teaching energy kids love.

That day he was telling stories about the medieval Tower of London, about the many people imprisoned, tortured, and killed there, their heads chopped off. He was being colorful and enjoying himself as he started talking about all the ghosts that were said to walk the Tower ramparts.

Jessica shot up her hand. "Mr. Bokor, do you believe in ghosts?"

Bokor beamed. "Do I believe in ghosts, Jessica? Absolutely. Memories are real, are they not? Well, memories are ghosts. Ghosts are memories. Does not history haunt us? The month of August is named for Augustus Caesar, the Roman Empire's first emperor. Thursday gets its name from Thor, the Nordic god of thunder. Oh yes, my friends, ancient gods—ghosts—are part our daily lives."

Bokor's words—echoes of my own thoughts—had me listening and watching intently. He must have caught that I was interested, because he wheeled about and barked, "Our new friend here, Tony, came from Connecticut. *Connecticut*: an Algonquian Indian word that means 'upon the long river.' Did you know that?"

I shook my head.

"My native land," he went on, "Haiti, takes its name from a Taino Indian word meaning 'land of high mountains.' So, ghosts of the old Caribbean world, lurking. Consider the name of our school and its founder, Mrs. Penda. I have no doubts her name comes from the last great Anglo-Saxon pagan king of what is now England.

"And," he boomed, "speaking of pagans, the school's big Halloween party is coming up. Anyone know the origin of Halloween?"

Rapt, no one spoke.

Bokor boomed on: "New Testament. Luke 9:60. 'Let the dead bury the dead.' But sometimes the dead are *not* buried. They wander.

"Indeed, those Anglo Saxons believed that those who had recently died hung about as ghosts and roamed the earth for seven years—*seven* years—until the very last day of that seventh year."

Into my head came Uncle Charlie's words: *Remember the number seven.*

Bokor went on. "What was *that* last day called? All Hallows' Eve. Guess how we changed that word? *Halloween*. It happens in two weeks, my friends. Right here.

"Yes, those ancient Anglo Saxons believed those seven-year-old ghosts had one last chance—Halloween eve—to regain life before plunging into the world of no return."

I felt as if Bokor was talking just to me. Same time I noticed he had no accent in his speech. How long, I wondered, had he been in America?

"Why do we wear masks on Halloween?" Bokor demanded. "To keep our identities hidden. Same reason we close the eyes of the dead. Somebody said: 'The eyes are the windows to the soul.' So, if *you* are being pursued by those ghosts—with their searching eyes—look out. Keep your eyes closed. But if you wear a mask it will keep that ghost from knowing who *you* are."

Mac called out, "Mr. Bokor, what happens if a ghost recognizes you?"

Bokor laughed. "Excellent question, Mac. If the ghost *does* recognize you, there is an exchange. The ghost rips out *your* soul, keeps it, and gains another seven years. But *you*, Mac, having lost your soul, join the ranks of wandering seven-year-spirits searching for another soul."

"Okay," said Jessica, "but what happens if the ghost doesn't recognize you?"

"Ah, yes. If, after seven years, the ghost *fails* to catch a living soul, he—or she—descends into oblivion, never to return."

Smiling broadly, Bokor looked around until his eyes fastened on me again. "Tony," he boomed. "You've come from afar. Know anyone who died recently?"

The whole class was staring at me, waiting for my answer. Uneasy, I shifted in my chair. In the far back row I saw the Penda Boy. He was looking right at me.

Flustered, I blinked because the boy had vanished, the way Uncle Charlie had done in the fog.

I felt a sharp poke on my shoulder. I swung about. Bokor loomed over me.

"Tony," Bokor cried, "you can learn that history is one long ghost story *if* you'll be good enough to look at me when I ask you a question. It's hard to miss *me*. Now, do you know anyone who died during the last year?"

With the eyes of the class on me, I stammered. "My . . . my great-uncle Charlie."

"Be careful," boomed Bokor. "Uncle Charlie's ghost might be after *your* soul."

The classroom hooted with laughter.

Bokor's remark cut me like a knife: Was the Uncle Charlie I kept seeing a ghost? It was bad enough that I was dealing with the Penda Boy's ghost. What if I was dealing with *two* ghosts, the Penda Boy *and* Uncle Charlie?

To my relief, the end-of-class-bell rang.

As if being chased, I hurried from class. Lilly caught up to me.

"So, Tony," she asked, full of smiles. "Do you believe in ghosts?"

I couldn't get Bokor's words out of my head. All I could answer was, "Maybe . . . sometimes."

She laughed. "Have you . . . ever seen one?"

I hesitated. Lilly was gazing up at me, waiting for a response. Suddenly wanting to talk about what had happened, I blurted, "I think I saw one this morning."

"No way," she said.

"Sort of. In that fog."

"Who was it?"

Not knowing how to explain, I stammered. "Ah . . . not sure."

Lilly cried, "Oh my God. I *love* that answer!" She held out an envelope. "Here's my party info. I love party cards! Still coming?" she asked.

"Sure."

"Awesome." She rushed off.

I watched her go. So different from Jessica. Ordinary. Nice. Without Jessica's forcefulness.

I opened her envelope. It was a printed card that read

YOU'RE INVITED TO A PARTY. Pictures of colorful parrots. The place and time filled in. It made me feel that I was becoming part of the school. It was the rest of the world that was hounding me.

I went back to thinking: *Two ghosts.*

Bokor had said, "Memories are ghosts. Ghosts are memories."

What was Uncle Charlie? What was the Penda Boy?

I felt like crying.

During lunch, I sat with Mia, Joel, Lilly, and Patrick. Mr. Bokor's talk had them babbling about the upcoming school Halloween party. I was learning that the event was truly big, an all-school affair. There was endless chatter about costumes they might wear.

I sat silently, caught up in the possibility of two ghosts stalking me.

Though I was only halfway through my lunch, I got up. "Have to go to see Mrs. Z," I announced.

She was at her desk, bent over work. As I approached, she looked up and offered a smile. "Hello, Tony. How nice to see you again. What can I do for you?"

"I'm supposed to tell you I want to be on the Ping-Pong team."

"Wonderful." She opened a drawer and pulled out a folder, then a sheet of paper. She looked up and handed me a paper with a sechedule. "Practice starts in November. Matches are already scheduled.

"Oh," she added. "Student clubs. Wednesday afternoon, last period. I assume Mr. Batalie gave you a list. You need to choose one."

"I will."

She looked at me severely. "You need to do that soon."

Paper in hand, I found myself staring at the painting of the boy. "Mrs. Z," I said, "I don't mean to bother you, but what . . . really happened to him?"

"The Penda Boy? I thought I told you. One day, apparently, he . . . disappeared. Students like to say it happened Halloween night."

"Did they ever find him?"

Mrs. Z's smile vanished. Her eyes showed fear. "I . . . don't believe so. All I know is that I don't want to meet him." She hauled back her smile. "But at the Halloween party, somebody always dresses up like him. You'll see him then. That's harmless." She gave a fake smile and, clearly not wanting to talk anymore, bent over her work.

I studied the boy's face. He didn't look harmless to me.

Then I peered over at the painting of Mrs. Penda. When

I'd first looked at it, I had thought she was angry. Now, as I gazed at it, she too seemed full of fear. Like the look in the Penda Boy's eyes. And on Ms. Foxton's face when I first met her. Batalie showed it too.

There was something in the school that frightened them all. I was frightened as well.

I'm glad to say nothing happened on Tuesday. But on Wednesday, since I had yet to pick a club, I had a free period at the end of the day. Batalie told me I could sit in on any club that interested me or go to the library. "But Tony," he said, the way Mrs. Z did, "you need to decide by next week."

I went to the library, which I had yet to visit. There was something that I wanted to check, something that Bokor had said about open eyes. When I had first seen Uncle Charlie outside the school, his eyes were open, as they had been when he died. At his funeral, they had been closed. Did that change mean anything? Would that help me understand what had happened in the fog?

The library was a huge room, with a vaulted ceiling braced by large wooden beams, and tall, narrow windows on one side. Heavy tables and chairs were lined up in two rows. Bookcases were filled with books, with the usual sections: fiction, science, picture books, and so on. A few students were there—I guess they had permission to skip clubs—reading and writing. The only sound was the turning of pages, as if the books were whispering secrets.

At the head of the room was a desk, piled with books and a computer. A woman was sitting there. When I approached, she looked up.

"Hello there," she said. "I don't think we've met. I'm Mrs. DuBois, the librarian."

"I'm Tony Gilbert. I'm new. Seventh grade."

"Welcome to the library, Tony. I'm always glad to meet new students. I hope you know we're open for an extra hour every day after classes."

She gestured to the room. "This was Mrs. Penda's private chapel. Looks medieval, doesn't it? I think it's beautiful."

"Yeah, nice."

"Can I help you with something?"

"Well . . . a few months ago, my uncle Charlie died. I was at the funeral."

"Oh dear, I'm so very sorry."

"And, he was in a . . . coffin. He looked okay, but they closed his eyes. I was sort of curious, you know, well, *why?* I mean, are dead people's eyes supposed to be closed . . . or open?"

To my relief, Mrs. DuBois said, "You know, I seem to recall

people used to put coins on a deceased person's eyes. Good for you. Customs like that are *so* interesting."

She stood up and beckoned me to follow her to the reference section, where she pulled out a book. It was titled *Superstitions: Meanings and Origins*.

I went to a table where no one else was sitting. The book's entries were arranged in alphabetical order: *Circle*, *Palmistry*, *Rabbit foot*. Each had an article, which explained the superstition and how it came to be.

I looked up *Eyes*, only to be referred to *Evil eyes*. Under *Evil eyes* there was a long entry, which ended with:

> *It was commonly believed that the eyes of dead people should be closed before they "saw" another person. If the eyes were open, the deceased might take that living person with them to the land of the dead.*

I read the paragraph a few times, thinking of the Penda Boy and the way he kept looking at me. I remembered too that when Uncle Charlie died, his eyes had stayed open. He *had* been looking at me.

What was it Bokor had told us? When a dead person's eyes are open and looking at you, the dead person is trying to grab your soul.

Hadn't Uncle Charlie said, "Hey, Tony, wouldn't it be great if you and I went to the other side, together?"

Dread was only half of what I felt.

For the rest of the time in school I remained watchful for sightings of the Penda Boy and Uncle Charlie, relieved to see neither. When school was over, I hurried home. Using my desk dictionary, I looked up the word *ghost*. The entry read:

Ghost: A soul or spirit

Ms. Foxton's words echoed in my head: *A friend is one soul in two bodies.* That made me remember something else Uncle Charlie had said: "Tony, when I die, I really want you to *join* me."

Were Uncle Charlie and the Penda Boy working together? Apart? Were they friends? *My* friends? Or were they both my enemies?

I walked my slackline. When you walk a slackline, the whole point is to walk, not think. I wanted emptiness. But, unable to stop thinking about ghost stuff, I kept falling.

As I lay on the floor, I saw Uncle Charlie watching me from a corner. I didn't know which I felt more, anger or fright. "You're not my memory!" I yelled at him. "You're a ghost. I'm not going with you."

He vanished.

I *had* to talk to Jessica. But not knowing how to explain it, I kept putting it off.

Wednesday morning, as I was leaving for school, Mom said, "We still need so much. I'm coming home early to do some shopping. Can you give me a hand?"

"Sure."

I went to school intending to talk to Jessica. I put it off again. It was like dodging the doctor, not because you're fearful you're sick, but because you worry the doc might tell you that you are *very* sick. In my case, I was afraid that Jessica would say that everything I dreaded was true. I decided—no—I was afraid—to talk to her. So I didn't, not all day.

But when I left school at three o'clock, Jessica, her black backpack slung over her shoulder, was right there at the bottom of the steps talking to Mac. It was as if, sensing what I was doing, she was going to make sure it was impossible for me to avoid her.

I told myself it was Jessica I needed to talk to, not Mac. I found him annoying and didn't understand their friendship. Short and pudgy, he followed her about like a plump ankle-biter dog, even though she was tall, trim, older-looking, self-assured.

Unsure what to do, I stood at the top of the school steps. Pretending I was listening to a message, I put my phone to my ear. All the while, I kept my eyes on Jessica.

She glanced around and offered her smile. I took the smile as saying something, that we two were connected in a special way. Then she must have told Mac to go off, because he went, waving good-bye to me.

Shoving my phone into a pocket, I came down the steps. Not that I intended to tell her about Uncle Charlie. She had nothing to do with him. It was the Penda Boy I needed help with.

"Hey," she called. "you didn't come to the club."

"I had something to do," I lied.

"When are we going to talk?"

Figuring I had no choice, I asked, "Have a good spot?"

"On Union," she said, adjusting her backpack. "There's a great yogurt place."

"Let's go."

We started downhill. Like so many of the city streets, it was extremely steep. Jessica said, "You don't like Mac."

She seemed to notice everything. I said, "He's okay."

"He likes hanging around me. Hey," she added, pushing hair away from her face, "those guys do what I tell them to do. You're a lot stronger."

Not knowing how to respond, but feeling I had to say something, I asked, "You live close?"

"The Richmond area. On Lake Street. In the morning, my mother drives me. End of day I take the bus home."

"What does your father do?"

"Who knows? In Boston with his new family. Almost never see him. You live just six blocks from the school, don't you?"

"An apartment," I said. "How did you know?"

She shrugged. "People talk."

What people?

I said, "Why do parked Frisco cars turn their wheels in, or out like that?"

"If their brakes fail, they won't roll down the hill and kill anyone."

I gave her a look.

"Happens. I was in an accident like that. I was okay, except I got my limp."

"That's amazing."

"It's an amazing city," said Jessica, smiling. "Maybe that's why I'm crazy. I was born here. Actually, I'm a distant relative of Mrs. Penda."

"The school's founder?" I said, glancing at her. I hadn't thought about it before, but recalling the painting of Mrs. Penda, I did notice a resemblance.

"Can you see it?" she said, registering my gaze. "You've been studying that painting of her."

"How do you know so much about me?"

"Mrs. Z. The school watchdog. She loves to gossip. Yeah, my family has lived here forever. In fact," she went on, "there's been at least one family member at the school since it began. That's why I haven't been kicked out."

"Why would they do that?"

"Because I ask questions."

"About what?"

"Those kids who disappeared from the school. Like Austin. The school's big secret. I tried talking to Ms. Foxton. Know what she said? If people learned about the kids who disappeared, the school would collapse.

"Oh, something you should know," Jessica said as we continued downhill. "All the kids who went missing were new."

"New what?"

"To the school. From way back, it always happens in seventh grade."

I stopped. "You mean . . . like me?"

She shrugged, looking at me with sympathetic eyes. I

turned away, upset but wanting to learn more.

We walked on without talking until I said, "Okay, I want to know. Was it Ms. Foxton who told you my uncle Charlie died?"

"Is *that* who it was? Your *uncle*? You must have been close, because like I told you, you stink of death."

I didn't know what to say.

"Hey," she said, bopping me on the arm, "some people are interested in life. I'm interested in death."

"How come?"

"It happens to everyone, right? But it's the one thing people want most to avoid. I know I do."

Feeling we were talking like real friends, I said, "There's something I haven't told you."

"What?"

"That old relative of yours, Mrs. Penda, she set up the school because her kid—the Penda Boy—died, right?"

"The first one to disappear."

I said, "In the school office, there's a painting of him."

"Obvious."

"But I'm pretty sure that kid I told you about, the one I saw in the tower, the kid in the painting, well, first day I came to class, he was sitting at the empty desk between you and Mac."

She halted, mouth slightly open, eyes fixed on me. With a nervous flick of her hand, she shoved hair from her face. "You saying . . . you saw the Penda Boy in . . . class? Next to *me*?"

I nodded. She was rattled, something I hadn't seen before.

"You . . . you ever see him again?" she asked.

"All over the school. Lots of times. Remember when Bokor was talking about ghosts, ghosts coming back and grabbing souls on Halloween? All of a sudden, he was *there*—sitting behind you, staring at me."

I could have sworn Jessica was trembling. "You sure?"

"Swear," I said, lifting a hand.

"Why didn't you tell me before?"

"Wasn't positive I was seeing him."

"You were."

"But how come I'm the only one seeing him?"

Without answering, Jessica started downhill again. It might seem strange, but I was glad she was upset. It was something we shared. Made me feel like I finally had a friend.

We arrived at the yogurt shop, got some, and sat down. From her backpack Jessica took out a pale blue tube of something, squirted out a pearl of it, and rubbed her hands and face with it.

"What's that?"

"Moisturizer. Keeps me young-looking."

"You're not exactly old."

"Told you. Don't intend to be. Okay," she said, putting the tube away, "want to know what I think? That kid you keep seeing, no question: he's the Penda Boy's ghost, and he's after you."

I put down my spoon. "Why me?"

"He wants your soul."

My stomach tightened. "What do you mean?"

"Like Bokor said. It's what happened to Austin. His kid brother died, so like you, Austin had death stink all over him. The Penda Boy grabbed him. Good-bye, Austin. With you, it's your uncle Charlie."

"What about him?"

"You were close, right? I keep telling you, you stink of his death. It attracts the ghost. Makes sense, doesn't it, dead liking dead. Accept it."

Wishing Uncle Charlie had stayed out of my life, I felt a spurt of anger. "What . . . what can I do?"

"Get rid of him, before he gets rid of you."

"But how . . . ," I stammered, "how . . . can I *get rid* of a ghost?"

Jessica leaned across the table. "Tony, just know that we— the Weird History Club—are *totally* on your side. The other kids, Barney and Mac, you don't like them. I know. But I'm in charge. You good with that?"

I sat there, not sure what to say.

"I need a guy like you," Jessica pressed. "Someone with brains." She flashed her smile. "We can do it."

"Do *what?*"

"Get rid of the Penda Boy."

"But he's dead."

"Tony, you heard Bokor: if his ghost gets you, he lives; you die."

I sat there, too terrified to speak.

She went on: "Look at the harm the Penda Boy has done. All those kids, disappearing. Austin was nice. But—a couple of weeks after school began—he disappeared."

"What . . . happened?" I whispered.

"Early on, Batalie was talking school rules. About no one being allowed in the towers. They *always* say that. All of a sudden, Austin—the new kid, right?—raises his hand. 'Mr. Batalie,' he says, 'I saw someone in the tower.'"

"I asked you guys if anyone else saw the ghost."

"Well . . . Austin. But he's not here anymore."

"What . . . what did Batalie say?"

"He said, 'Not possible.' But a few days later . . . Austin's gone."

I said, "I saw someone in the tower."

"My point."

"Did anyone look for Austin?"

"Sure. But no luck. *Disappeared.* But then, guess what?"

"What?"

"School said no one should talk about it. 'Keep it in the family.' Penda kids lap up that junk. Sucky school spirit. Tony, I'm telling you, if we don't do something, what happened to Austin will happen to you. You're going to disappear too."

I was finding it hard to breathe.

She said, "I'm glad you told me about what's going on. Want some advice? Don't tell anyone else around the school. They'll think you're nuts."

"I guess so. . . ."

"Know why the club wears black ties and neck scarves?"

I shook my head.

"To honor the missing kids. It tells people *we* haven't forgotten. First time I saw you, I was worried about you."

"Why?"

"I keep telling you. I knew right off you were connected to someone who died. At Penda, that's not good."

"People say to stay away from you."

"Sure, because they care more about the school's reputation than about missing kids." She leaned closer. "You know how it is," she said. "When kids tell the truth, grown-ups never want to listen. They want us dumb. Under control. Hey, girls especially should follow rules. Do what they're told. Be sweet. Big eyes for the boys. Right?"

"I guess."

"I'm smarter than they want. And I'm pretty. I know that. That makes it worse. People do *not* like pretty and smart in the same girl. Does it bother you?"

"No. I just want to know what to do."

"Join our club. We'll protect you and get the Penda Boy. And if we get rid of him, it'll be great for the school. Accept it: The Penda Boy is the enemy. I'm your friend."

"Thanks," I muttered.

"Tony," she pushed, "I'm *trying* to help you."

"I know, but I have to do something soon."

"I'll come up with a plan," she said, offering her smile. "Promise. Save you, save the school." She grabbed my arm, gave it a shake. As she did, I noticed her ring, with the seven stones on it.

Trying to find something to say, I blurted out, "How come you have those black stones on your ring?"

"They're onyx. Seven of them. Onyx is for self-control and protection, and seven because that's the most important number in the universe."

That was what Uncle Charlie had said right before he died.

"Seven is magic," Jessica said. "I read somewhere that the old Greeks thought it was a perfect number. In the Bible, it took seven days to make the world. In fact, *seven* is in the Bible more than any other number. True. Ever notice phone numbers always had just seven numbers? Ever hear of the Masons? A huge secret society. Seven is big to them. My name has seven letters. Seven protects me. Hey, I'm a *seventh* grader. This is my big year."

I was getting increasingly tense. It wasn't only *what* she said. It was her constant pushing, her insisting I *do* something, but she never made it exactly clear *what*. Same time, I kept telling myself, *She's trying to help me. She's my friend.* I had to listen.

My cell phone rang. I pulled it from my pocket. It was my mom. "'Lo."

Mom said, "I'm here, home. Where are you?"

"Down on Union. In a yogurt shop, with a friend."

"Nice. Remember? We were going shopping. Think you could get back soon?"

I looked across the table. Jessica was waiting for me. I admit I was glad to have the excuse to go, to think, to calm down.

"Yeah," I said into the phone. "I'll come." I stood up.

"Gotta go?" said Jessica, sounding disappointed.

"My mom," I said, trying to say it as if *I* was disappointed.

"Hey, if kids got rid of their parents, things would be more fun, right?" Her smile was almost a smirk. "Don't worry," she said. "We'll talk more. We're a team, right? I'll work on a plan."

"Yeah, sure."

I started out of the yogurt shop.

"Tony," she called. "Trust me."

"Right," I replied, because I did want to trust her. But that, I remembered, was what Uncle Charlie had asked me to do just before he died.

As I climbed the steep hill toward home, I kept telling myself I had to accept the fact that the Penda Boy was after me. That the only person making sense, the only one helping me, was Jessica. No sooner did I have that thought than I saw Uncle Charlie across the street.

My frustration flipped. I shouted, "Family was always saying, 'What's the deal with Uncle Charlie?' You're my enemy, that's what. Go away."

He vanished. *Good.*

I started walking again. Jessica's talk about *seven* plowed into my head. I counted the letters of my name—Anthony.

Seven. I was in seventh grade. Too weird. What was it that Dad had said about *weird*? It didn't just mean strange but also fate.

I had asked, "Whose?"

"Yours, I guess," Dad had said, laughing.

I labored up the hill. I wasn't laughing. I was petrified.

When I got home, Mom was at the kitchen table making a shopping list. "Hi. Sorry to pull you away. Who's your friend?"

"Some girl from class."

"Oh, nice," said Mom, trying to act uninterested. "Look over my list while I get ready. See if I forgot anything."

She went to get her purse. I picked up the list but didn't look at it. I kept thinking, *If the Penda Boy and Uncle Charlie are against me, who's on my side?* The same answer always came: Jessica.

Mom and I went out together. After a while I said, "I've been invited to a party on Friday night."

"Lovely. What's the occasion?"

"Some girl in my class. It's her birthday. She's turning thirteen."

Mom worked hard not to grin. "That the girl you were with?"

"No. Different."

She allowed herself to smile. "You're becoming quite the ladies' man."

I frowned, but what she said made me feel good.

Next day, during lunch, I sat with a bunch of classmates that included Lilly. There was a lot of laughing, giggling, and teasing as they talked about the Halloween party.

"So awesome," said a boy named Mark. "So much more fun than Christmas."

"Everyone comes to school in costume," explained Lilly, who had sat down next to me. "Teachers too. Even Ms. Foxton. I love her. Mr. Bokor always comes as a warlock. So cool."

Abruptly, the room began to shake. *Earthquake*, I realized. During the time it lasted—three, four seconds—everyone froze. The instant it stopped, as if nothing had happened, Joel said, "I'm going to be Henry the Eighth. Anyone want to be one of my wives?"

"No way" came a chorus of laughing voices.

Was I the only one who'd felt the earthquake? The way I was the only one who saw the Penda Boy?

"I'll be the fisherman from *The Old Man and the Sea*," said a kid named Carlos.

Ian said, "Who's going to be the dead fish?"

Laughter.

Mia, Lilly's best friend, said, "I've got this great clown outfit," and then Ian announced, "I'm going to be the Penda Boy."

Groans. "So lame," called Peter. "The Penda Boy is always there."

I asked myself if it would be the ghost, or someone costumed as the boy.

Lilly turned to me. "Have any idea what you'll be?"

From across the cafeteria I saw Jessica's eyes on me, her look full of mockery. I was sure she was reminding me that the kids I was with had no idea what was happening with the Penda Boy.

I realized that all the kids at the table were waiting for my answer.

"Hey, Tony," called Todd, "anyone ever told you how spacey you are?"

"That means he's going to dress up as an astronaut!" shouted Lee, who always made puns.

The kids moaned in appreciation as the end-of-lunch bell rang. Leaving the cafeteria, Lilly was at my side. "Still coming to my birthday party?"

"Sure," I said, only wanting to have some fun.

❖ ❖ ❖

In history class, Bokor talked about what he called "the Black Death." He described it as a deadly plague that swept through Europe in the fourteenth century.

"Historians who have studied this," he said as he paced about the room, "are not sure if half or a third of the European population died. In a matter of *months*. All these deaths within such a short period. People high and low. Try to visualize it. They just ceased to exist."

His voice boomed with fervor.

"Whole villages, towns, cities, emptied," he cried in dramatic fashion. "Think of your classmates—disappearing. Here today, gone tomorrow. Imagine it. Look around."

I was afraid to.

"Tony," Bokor called. "You're not looking."

I turned and saw Jessica watching me. Behind her—I was sure she didn't know—was the Penda Boy, eyes full of pleading. All I could do was gape.

"That's enough staring, Tony," I heard.

I swung around. Bokor was hovering over me. "Tony. You look like you actually saw a dead person."

The class laughed.

But I *had* seen someone—someone who'd died a hundred years ago.

Too tossed to think, I couldn't wait until the end-of-class bell rang. As kids got up and left the room, Bokor called out, "Tony Gilbert. Will you please stay?"

I remained at my desk, nervous that Bokor was going to ask me what I had seen.

With a small grunt, he eased his bulk into a chair behind his desk. "Tony," he began, "I realize that you and I haven't truly spoken—which, since you are new, I should have done so. I must apologize. Anyway, here's a belated welcome to Penda. Things going well?"

"Guess so."

He smiled. "Enjoying history?"

I lifted a shoulder. "It's okay."

"In your former school did you have much history?"

"American Revolution."

He laughed. "East Coast history. By the time the Pilgrims landed on Plymouth Rock, the University of Mexico was almost a hundred years old. I'm hoping you already know," he went on, more seriously, "but I thought I should give a reminder: seventh graders have a research paper due at the end of October. Halloween. That's soon.

"What I am interested in is your learning the *idea* of historical research. Learning about sources—primary and secondary. Footnotes. Bibliography. I'm not so concerned about the subject you write about, but it's a good idea to take on a topic that interests you. Have you ever done anything like that before?"

I shook my head.

"Since you've come from the East Coast, maybe you'd like to learn about Spanish California, or San Francisco's great 1906 earthquake, or . . ." He paused. "What about the Penda School? I know a lot about it. Be glad to help you."

I heard him, but I was thinking about the Penda Boy.

"Anyway, we can talk, but you need to take on a doable project. Time is short. Your classmates have already chosen topics. Thanks for staying. Feel free to come by any time."

Relieved it was normal school stuff, I said, "Thank you," and left.

When I stepped from class, Jessica was waiting. "What was that about?" she asked.

"The history term paper. Have to choose a topic."

"No, when Bokor asked everyone to look around, there was the strangest expression on your face."

I hesitated.

Jessica shoved her hair back. "You saw the Penda Boy, didn't you?"

Not wanting to talk, I moved down the hall.

She grabbed my arm. "Tell me."

"He was sitting behind you."

"What . . . was he doing?"

"Just . . . sitting there."

"Was he looking at you? Me?"

"I'm not sure. At lunch," I asked, "did you feel an earthquake?"

She scowled. "I don't pay attention to them."

The class bell rang.

"We're late for science," I said, glad to hurry on.

Jessica, staying close, said, "Something you should know: Bokor is the Weird History Club adviser."

"Okay."

She grabbed me again. "Tony, the Penda Boy is after you. You've got to *do* something. It's almost Halloween. I want to help you."

"I know," I said, and scooted toward science class.

We were almost at the room when a voice rang out. "Jessica. Tony."

It was Ms. Foxton, and she did not look happy. "The class bell has already rung," she said, coming up to us. "Shouldn't you two be in class?"

Already befuddled, and now cowed by her sharpness, I stammered, "I . . . I was talking to Mr. Bokor."

"Did he give you a late pass?"

"No."

"Jessica, what excuse do you have?"

Jessica stood there, glaring. "I was waiting for Tony. He's my friend."

"So I have been informed," said Ms. Foxton with a frown. "Where is your next class?"

"Science," said Jessica. "Right here."

"Please, both of you. Get where you belong."

I opened the classroom door. As I did, I looked back at Ms. Foxton. There was fright in her eyes. I had no doubt: she was afraid of Jessica. And as I stepped into class, Jessica muttered, "Someday I'm going to have to kill that woman."

She sounded as if she meant it.

That night, after dinner, I sat at my desk and checked the internet earthquake site Dad had told me about, the one that listed the day's earthquakes all over the world. There were a lot. *None* in San Francisco. But I was sure I had felt one at the school. Once again I asked myself, was I the only one who noticed it, the way I was the only one to see the Penda Boy? And this time I had a new thought: Was there a connection?

As I sat at my desk, trying to think it out, Mom walked in.

Without saying a word, she sat behind me on my bed. She said, "Tony, love, I need to talk to you. Please look at me."

Sensing trouble, I swiveled around.

"Late this afternoon," she began, "at work, I had a call from Ms. Foxton. The first thing she said was that your teachers are enjoying having you in class."

"That's not why she called you."

"True. She said she found you socializing in the hallway when you should have been in science class."

"That's bull!" I cried, instantly angry. "Mr. Bokor, the history teacher, asked me to stay after class to talk about some paper I have to write."

"And?"

"I did. I just forgot to ask him for a late note. And I went right from his class to science. Why would Ms. Foxton even call you about something so stupid?"

"She said that since you're new, it's important to get off to a good start. I guess a good start for her includes your knowing and following school rules. She was sure Mr. Batalie provided you with the rules. Did you read them?"

"That's so unfair." I turned my back on her.

Mom said, "There was another reason she called."

I slumped over my desk. "What?"

"When she found you, you were with another student. A

girl named Jessica Richards."

"What's Jessica got to do with it?"

"Ms. Foxton doesn't have much good to say about the girl. Has she become a . . . special friend of yours?"

"Just tell me what she said."

"The girl seems to create problems in the school."

"So Ms. Foxton is telling you who my friends should be."

"Tony, one of the advantages and, yes, disadvantages of a school like Penda is that they keep very close watch over students. They don't hesitate to communicate with parents. I, for one, appreciate it. I think Ms. Foxton means well."

I said, "Everybody hates her. I can make my own friends."

"Well, you needed to know what she said."

"Fine."

"Ms. Foxton gave me her private number. She said you could call her if you wanted to talk about what happened. Or anything else that's troubling you."

Mom stood up, leaned over me, put down a yellow sticky note with Ms. Foxton's number on it, and hugged me. "We simply want you to be happy, do well, and enjoy school. We came here in large measure because of you."

Breaking free, I said, "You came because you and Dad got better jobs."

"Tony, we *all* needed a change, and your uncle Charlie left money because he wanted you to go to Penda."

"I hate Uncle Charlie."

Her face showed surprise. "Well . . . that's a change."

I said, "Happens."

I slammed the door after her, then sat at my desk, furious with Ms. Foxton. If she wanted me to drop Jessica as a friend, there was no way I was going to do it. Jessica was the one person helping me.

I stuffed Ms. Foxton's phone number among the pages of the book I was reading, snapped the book shut, and grabbed the black tie and put it on. I didn't do it right, but it was on. Then I walked the slackline but kept falling.

Next morning, as Dad was tying on my black tie, he said, "History club today?"

"Not exactly."

"What's the club do?"

"Study history."

"Recent? Ancient? Local?"

"Local."

As I was about to leave the apartment, Mom said, "You have a birthday party tonight, right? What's involved?"

"Not much."

Mom hesitated and then asked, "Is it that Jessica Richards

who is having the party?"

"No."

"May I ask who?"

"Lilly, if you have to know."

Mom eased up. "Do you need to get a birthday present?"

"Don't know what she'd like."

"Would you like me to pick up a gift card?"

"Thanks," I snapped, as if I were doing Mom a favor.

Since I was wearing the black tie to school for the first time, but not wanting to make a big entrance, I got to homeroom early. Only a few students were there, but that included Jessica. She looked up, saw my tie, and rewarded me with a great smile. *She's my one real friend*, I thought as I sat down next to her.

She said, "I knew you were smart."

Hearing the remark, a couple of nearby kids turned and looked at my tie and me. There was disapproval on their faces. I didn't care.

"We'll talk at recess," I said to Jessica, and made a point of staying next to her.

Batalie came up to where I was sitting and said, "Tony, Mr. Bokor would like you to drop in to see him during recess." He paused and then said, "You're wearing a black tie."

Expecting more displeasure, all I said was, "I guess."

"Ah," he said, with a grin, which was rare for him. "An interesting choice."

"I like it," I said.

"The best reason," he said. Returning to his desk, he made an agitated fuss over some papers. I wished I knew what he was thinking.

When the midmorning recess bell rang, I turned to Jessica. "Have to go see Bokor. Catch you at lunch."

I was sure I knew why Bokor had asked me to come—that late note he'd failed to give. Certain he was going to blame me, I went down the hall as slowly as I could, telling myself not to lose my temper.

When I got to Bokor's room, he looked around. "Tony. Thanks for dropping by. I think I owe you an apology."

Surprised, I just stood there.

He went on: "Yesterday I asked you to stay after class to talk about your term paper. Then I forgot to give you a late pass for your next class. I gather you informed Ms. Foxton, who found you in the hall on the way to science. Apparently, she didn't believe you. Penda has a lot of rules," he said with a smile full of sympathy. "I've already told Ms. Foxton it was my fault. Sorry for any unpleasantness."

I was astonished. In all my years at school, no teacher had ever apologized to me. All I could manage to get out was "Thanks."

Bokor said, "We'll chalk it up to experience, mine and yours. Can you accept that?"

"Sure," I said, and turned to go.

"Oh, Tony. Have you chosen a topic for your paper?"

I shifted back around.

"We're getting closer to the deadline," he said. "May I urge you to do a brief history of the Penda School? I know a fair bit about it and can guide you to all kinds of sources. It'll save you time. I even have the original building plans for the mansion, before it was a school. I would enjoy working with you. Getting to know you. It might be a fun project. The real point is, Halloween—the due date—is almost here."

The offer, I was sure, was part of his apology. Thankful, I said, "Sure. I'll try."

"Wonderful. The sooner we meet to get you started the better. Today's Friday. How about meeting after school on Monday? Does that work for you?"

"Think so."

"See you then."

By the time I got to the cafeteria, recess was almost over. As I grabbed a jelly doughnut and OJ, the bell rang. Since students were not allowed to take food out of the cafeteria, I bolted everything down. As I did, Jessica came up to me.

"What was Bokor all about?"

"He apologized for not giving me a late note yesterday—you know, when Ms. Foxton found us in the hall. She called my mother."

"What for?"

"To warn her about you."

Alarm filled her face. "Did you say anything?"

"Told her I could have my own friends."

She gave me a great smile. "See. You're terrific. And I think I've worked out a plan. You know," she said, her voice low. "How to get rid of the Penda Boy. You're coming to the club meeting at lunch, right?"

"Right," I called after her as she hurried away.

I headed back to class, realizing I was feeling better than I had in a long time. And it was Jessica who was making me feel that way.

At noon, as I went toward the cafeteria to meet with the club, I caught sight of the Penda Boy. He was alone. Wanting to avoid him, I reversed my direction and ducked among a group of kids. Annoying, but it was a reminder that I needed to do two things: get away from him and get rid of him.

I got some lunch and joined Jessica, Mac, and Barney at the club table. When I sat down, Jessica wasted no time. "Okay," she announced, "as of now Tony is a full member of the Weird History Club."

"Way to go," said Mac.

Barney held up a hand for a high five. It was like slapping soft butter.

"Only rule," Jessica said to me. "Every day wear something black."

I grinned and flapped my tie. "I'm good."

Jessica gave me one of her big smiles but quickly became serious when she said, "Okay. Here's the thing: the Penda Boy is after Tony."

Mac put his hand to his mouth and nibbled the side of his thumbnail. "What's he doing?" he said.

Jessica said, "So far, only stalking him. Anyway, it's obvious: he's waiting to grab Tony's soul. Like with Austin's."

Mac said, "Uh-oh."

Barney, watery eyes blinking, added, "Not good."

I thought, *How come they aren't more surprised?*

"Our job," Jessica went on, "is to do two things. First, protect Tony. Right?"

"Right," echoed Mac.

"Second," Jessica went on, "get rid of the Penda Boy."

"It's about time," said Barney.

"Totally," said Mac.

I said, "Has anyone ever tried to?"

The boys looked to Jessica. She said, "If they have, it didn't work, did it?"

"Nope," said Barney.

"Where," I said, "do you think . . . he is?"

Mac said, "You told us you saw him watching you from the high tower, right?"

"First time I visited the school."

Mac said, "Well, people say that's where—long time ago— he disappeared."

"Somewhere up there," agreed Barney.

Mac looked at Jessica. She gave a small nod, after which he said, "Which means, for sure, to nail him, we're going to have to get into the towers."

I said, "How do you do that?"

Barney said, "There are doors all over the place."

"Aren't they sealed?" When no one replied, I said, "Anyone ever try to open them?"

Mac, biting a fingernail, glanced at Jessica.

She said, "I can do it."

Remembering what Ms. Foxton had told me, I said, "But I thought if you get caught in the towers, you're in big trouble with the school."

"We can duck that," said Jessica.

I said, "How?"

"Here's my idea," said Jessica. "Big Halloween party is coming up, right?"

"Right," echoed Barney.

"Everyone will be in costume," Jessica went on. "With all those costumes and masks, no one knows who anyone is." She looked around. "True?"

"True," agreed Mac.

Barney nodded.

Jessica said: "Okay, then the Halloween party is the perfect time to sneak into the towers, because with everyone in costume, nobody will know what we're doing."

That made me remember what Bokor had said, how masks were the way to hide from your enemy.

"I like that," said Mac.

"Cool," said Barney.

"'Course," Jessica hurried on, "we'll know what costumes we're in, so we can work together."

"Great," said Barney.

Jessica sat back as if she had worked it all out. She turned to me. "What do you think?"

They were looking at me as if I was the one who was deciding. I said, "Sure, get into the towers, but then, if we find the Penda Boy, he's a ghost, so how do we deal with him?"

Jessica said, "I'll work it out. First thing is, find him."

To me, Mac said, "And you're the only one who sees him."

To which Barney added, "And the big tower is where he lives."

"Guess who knows most about the school?" said Jessica. "I mean the way it's built and all."

"Bokor," Mac answered.

I said, "My term paper is about the history of the Penda School. Bokor said he'd help me. Said he'd show me the plans for the school."

Jessica gave me a good smile. "There—you figured it out. Bet Bokor will tell you everything you need to know. Maybe lend you the plans."

Barney offered another high five. "Tony, you're a genius."

For a moment no one spoke. Then Jessica said, "We all in?"

They were waiting for me.

"In," I heard myself say.

"Good-bye, Penda Boy," muttered Barney. He actually giggled.

The end-of-lunch bell rang. The boys rushed off. As Jessica

got up to go, she said, "You were terrific."

I remained, staring at my hands, not certain I knew what I had agreed to, only that it had happened fast. As to what, exactly, we'd *do* once we got hold of the Penda Boy's ghost—how we were going to kill him—that hadn't been said.

Alone, I walked back to class, mulling over what happened. Something bothered me: a feeling that everyone in the Weird History Club—Mac, Barney, and even Jessica—was saying lines like in some TV sitcom. Rehearsed. Fake. As if they knew what Jessica was going to say, knew what *they* were going to say. Talking about sneaking into the towers. About me being the only one who saw the ghost. About Bokor knowing about those towers. About me having just met with him. A coincidence? All the same, I did believe that the Penda Boy was a ghost. And that he was after me.

I didn't like Barney and Mac. But Jessica was solid. If bad things happen, go to strong people for protection, right? She was my friend. Her plan about using costumes as disguises was clever. That part made me feel good.

Then why, I asked myself, did that conversation make me uneasy? Because her talk about *doing* something about the Penda Boy was vague. Besides all that, it seemed it was mostly *me* who was to do the doing.

And I still didn't know *what* I was supposed to do.

At the end of the day, as I left science class, Jessica was waiting. "I want to show you something," she said.

We headed down the hall, where she pointed to a spot on the wall. It was a small circle in the wood, colored a bit differently from the rest of the panel. "What's that?" I asked.

"A filled-in hole," said Jessica. "Get it? From an old doorknob. This panel used to be a door. See? It's narrower than the panels next to it. They are all over the place. Sealed. There's even one in our homeroom. Bet it goes to a tower. All we have to do is pry it open."

"How are we going to do that?"

"Knife. Chisel."

"Break it open?" I said, uneasy.

"You want to get the ghost, don't you?"

"Sure," I muttered, but my discomfort made me want to go home. "Have a nice weekend," I said, and turned away.

"Hey," she called.

I stopped.

"Enjoy your party," she said with a smile.

She seemed to know everything.

I came down one of the central stairways. On the other

steps, the Penda Boy was standing there, watching me. Avoiding looking at him, I wondered if he knew what we were planning to do.

A better question was, did I?

On the street, Lilly was waiting with a bunch of her friends. "Tony!" she called. "Party at five!"

"I know," I said, glad for the reminder of the time because my head was so muddled I had forgotten.

As I walked home, I called my mother and told her I had to be at Lilly's party at five.

"We'll get you there," she told me. "Oh, I picked up a gift card."

"Thanks."

"Here's a nice thing," she added. "Ms. Foxton called me and told me you were right—being late for class *was* the history teacher's fault."

"Told you."

"But think about it, Tony. The school made a mistake, and they were big enough to admit it. That's not common. Ms. Foxton is a nice, honest person."

"Yeah, right," I said, hoping she heard my sarcasm.

"I gave you her number. You *could* call her and say thanks."

I had no intention of calling Ms. Foxton, but as I went

home, I had to admit she was acting okay. But I was equally sure it was only because Bokor had gone to her. Maybe I could tell Bokor about the Penda Boy. I felt I could trust him. He had talked about memories and ghosts, so he might understand. And he was the adviser to the Weird History Club.

In fact, except for the Penda Boy, things were going well. I had gotten rid of Uncle Charlie's ghost. Now all I had to do was get rid of the Penda Boy.

I'm going to do it, I told myself. *I am.*

My parents came home early, more excited about Lilly's party than I was. Lots of smiles and knowing nods.

"Who else will be there?" "Tell us about Lilly." Their questions were irritating, because I had no answers.

Dad offered a cab, but when I mapped Lilly's address on my phone, I saw that she lived only twelve blocks away, so I went on my own. I brought a birthday gift card from H&M clothing store (whatever that was), which Mom had bought. I hoped it was okay.

Lilly and her family lived in the second-floor apartment of an old Victorian three-decker. It reminded me of a gingerbread house, complete with colored frosting. She had invited ten kids, half boys, half girls, plus her sister, a fourth grader who also went to Penda. Lilly's parents were there too. Younger than my parents.

In the large living room—bookcases filled with books against the walls, along with real paintings in frames—there were balloons on the ceiling and a dangling string of colored letters spelling out *Lilly—Teenager at Last.*

We kids arrived around the same time. There was lots of laughing, joking, and fooling around. Lilly was very excited. Sometimes the girls all ran off together, leaving the boys to accidentally pop balloons. I wasn't sure how I felt: One moment I was a little kid, and enjoying it. Then I thought about Jessica and the Penda Boy and I was living in a different world from everyone else.

We walked to a movie, with Lilly's parents going along to pay for tickets. When the movie was over, her parents were waiting for us. Calmer, we went back to Lilly's place, where we had pizza, soda, and a birthday cake. Lilly paid a lot of attention to me. I was having a good time.

After food, we sang "Happy Birthday" and sat in front of a large flat-screen TV, which no one watched. There was school gossip, plus talk about the upcoming Halloween party. That made me think about the Weird History Club and going after the Penda Boy.

During a lull in the chatter, I said, "Hey, do any of you guys know what happened to that Austin kid? You know, because he was gone, I got into Penda."

Instantly, the mood in the room changed. The kids became quiet, uneasy, eyeing one another.

It was Mia—Lilly's best friend—who said, "We were told not to talk about it."

"Who told you?"

Joel said, "Batalie and Foxton."

Wanting to find out how much they knew about Austin, I said, "But if all of you know what happened, that means I'm the only one here who doesn't."

Lilly said, "True."

They were stealing nervous glances at one another.

I said, "He disappeared, right?"

"Disappeared?" cried Patrick. "Who told you *that?*"

"That's what I heard."

"No way."

Puzzled, I said, "Then . . . what happened?"

The kids kept glancing at one another.

It was Lilly who said, "Why can't Tony know? *We* know. It's not like we're in school."

They squirmed. I waited impatiently.

"Well," began Lilly. "Austin had—"

"Oh my God . . . ," whispered Mia. "Don't."

"Tell me," I pushed.

They were silent a while longer until Lilly said, "I think Tony should know."

The other kids sat there, looking uncomfortable.

"Okay," said Lilly. "I'm telling."

"Austin had a younger brother," Lilly began. "And, you know, older brother, younger brother. Close. Anyway, I don't know what happened, but the kid got sick. Not sure with what. Something nasty. "

"Thing is," said Mia softly, "the boy . . . died."

"Fast," added Madison.

"Really sad," said Philip.

"Ghastly," said Lilly.

"When did it happen?" I asked.

"Last spring. Before Austin came to Penda."

I said, "So he was new to the school."

They nodded and kept glancing at one another, increasingly jumpy.

"Go on," I urged.

"Okay," said Philip. "Then, when school started, what people say is that Jessica and that club of hers . . ." He trailed off.

Madison went on. "Right. Jessica found out about Austin's brother. Don't know how. She and her Weird History Club told Austin—" She stopped speaking.

Lilly blurted out, "They told Austin that his brother was *not* dead. That . . . that he was in one of the towers."

"In the towers?" I echoed.

"Which," said Philip, "was nuts."

Lilly said, "People say Jessica told Austin that the Penda Boy was up there—I mean, the Penda Boy's ghost—and that the ghost was holding Austin's brother prisoner. Trying to take his soul."

I was feeling increasingly uneasy.

"Talk about *weird*," said Joel.

Austin's story went on, bouncing from kid to kid.

"Like, people always joke about a ghost in the towers. Not true, duh, but Austin believed it. Even said he *saw* the ghost."

"He freaked, totally."

"Kept talking about how his brother was not completely dead. That he needed to find him in the towers and kill the Penda Boy's ghost so he could rescue his brother."

"People say that Jessica—and her stupid club—told Austin she would help him get into the towers so he could get rid of the Penda Boy's ghost and save his brother. That he should do it at Halloween."

"*This* Halloween," threw in Philip.

I listened, breathless.

"Only Austin couldn't wait. He tried to open one of the old doors and get into the towers on his own."

"He was caught trying."

"Strict school rules about that. There was talk about expelling him."

"Before it could happen, Austin's family learned what Jessica had been telling him. They got so upset they pulled Austin out of school and actually moved to Seattle or someplace."

"I guess his parents were furious with the school, saying that Austin was being bullied by Jessica and her friends. They say the parents were going to sue the school."

"So we were asked not to say anything about Austin, or Jessica, because, I guess, you know, legal stuff."

I said, "Did . . . did anyone ask Jessica about it?"

"Sure, but she *claimed* she never spoke to Austin about his brother. Said she didn't know *anything* about the Penda Boy. Said she didn't even *believe* in ghosts. Same for the other lame Weird History Club kids."

"No proof at all that she did . . . except Austin, and he was, you know, gone."

"And, hate to say it, but a little crazy too."

"So the school agreed, when Austin left—we all agreed—not to say anything."

"For the good of Penda."

"And that," said Lilly, "is what happened."

Astonished, I sat there, stupefied, trying to make sense of it all. What I had just heard was so utterly different from what Jessica had told me about Austin. *Except* the parts about going into the towers and getting rid of the Penda Boy's ghost. And the business of trying to take souls, like Bokor had said. And . . . Jessica *did* know a lot about the Penda Boy. She *did* believe in the ghost.

"I felt so bad for Austin and his family," said Lilly.

Mia said, "Tony, you have to promise not to say anything. The school would really get upset."

I said, "*Did* . . . did anyone look in the towers?"

"You can't!" cried Patrick. "The doors are all sealed off. The school even resealed the one Austin tried to open."

Eyeing me, waiting for my response, the kids became quiet. I was too shocked to speak.

Joel poked me. "You hear anything different?"

I started to say, "Well, Jessica . . ."

Mia rolled her eyes.

"No offense, Tony," Philip cut in, "but Jessica is like, absolutely, totally . . . wacko with a capital *W*."

"She says *insane* things."

"You can't *ever* believe her."

There was an awkward silence until Philip said, "Yeah, Tony, you're smart. You had on their black tie. That mean you joined her Wednesday club? How come?"

I couldn't respond.

Lilly said, "Tony, promise you won't tell Jessica what we said. She'd kill us."

"She really would," agreed Mia.

I think I may have nodded.

For a moment no one spoke. Lilly rescued me. "Oh my God!" she cried. "I forgot to open my presents."

There was a mad scramble into another room. While Lilly opened gifts, the business of Austin, Jessica, and the Weird History Club was forgotten.

Not by me. According to these kids, the story was all about Jessica wanting Austin to go into the towers to get the Penda Boy, which was exactly what she wanted me to do. Austin to save his brother. Me to save myself. Except these kids didn't believe in the ghost. I did.

At about ten thirty, parents began to arrive. The boys went home. The girls were staying for a sleepover.

"Are your parents coming?" Lilly's father asked me when I was the only boy remaining.

"I can walk."

"Where do you live?"

When I told him, he said, "Come on. I could use a walk. I'll take you."

At the door, Lilly gushed a good-bye. "Thanks *so* much for coming. Your gift was so generous. I *love* H&M."

"Sure."

I headed home with her father.

He said, "Lilly told us you recently started at Penda. Are things going well?"

"It's fine."

"Recently moved to San Francisco?"

"Uh-huh."

"Like it?"

"So far."

"Lilly says nice things about you."

"Thanks."

"Excited about the school Halloween party?"

"Guess."

"I promise: it won't be like any Halloween you've ever experienced before."

That was exactly what was chewing at me.

When I got home, my parents had all kinds of questions about the party. I didn't tell them much. Instead, I went to my room and flung myself onto my bed. The story about Austin the kids had told me was so different from what Jessica had said. But since Lilly and her friends *all* agreed, it was hard to argue with them.

Why would Jessica tell me such a *different* story?

What did Austin and I have in common? We were both new to the school. Both in the seventh grade. His brother had died. Austin was unhappy about it. Uncle Charlie had died. I was unhappy about that. The kids said there was no ghost. Austin said he had seen the ghost. I had seen him too. Many times. He *was* a ghost. I was sure of it. He *was* stalking me. Had he stalked Austin?

I reached for my phone and was about to call Jessica when I changed my mind. It was late. Eleven thirty. Her mother might object to my calling. My mom would. The next day was Saturday. No school. If I went to her house, I could judge her reaction—face-to-face—about what I'd heard. Just the two of us. Hey, she was my friend. I owed her. "Trust me," she had said, and I really wanted her to explain away what I'd heard.

According to the school directory, she lived at 1520 Lake Street, only about thirty blocks away. My GPS app gave me directions. Not that far.

I'd go.

❖ ❖ ❖

Saturday morning, a little after nine, I told my parents I needed to get a special notebook for school down on Union Street. Instead, I headed for Jessica's home. The closer I got, the more tense I became, worried how Jessica would react. Sensing she wasn't a person you'd want to get angry, I was hoping she wouldn't be annoyed. I reminded myself that I'd promised I wouldn't tell Jessica what the kids had said about Austin. I'd say Ms. Foxton had told me. Jessica hated her anyway.

There was nothing special about Lake Street. A quiet, wide street, with evenly spaced trees on sidewalks and not many people around. The usual parked cars. As for the house numbered 1520, it looked like other houses on the street, maybe smaller, simpler. Certainly not old or fancy like Lilly's place.

I walked up some tiled steps to a windowed door, its inside covered by white lace. I took a deep breath, hoped I was doing the right thing, reminded myself that Jessica was my friend, and pushed the doorbell.

A shadow loomed behind the window. The door opened. A slight, gray-haired woman stood there, holding a book in hand, her finger wedged in the place she probably was reading.

"Yes?" she said in a soft voice. "May I help you?"

"Hi," I said. "I'm here to see Jessica."

The woman's face turned quizzical. "Jessica?"

"Jessica Richards. She goes to the Penda School. I'm in her class. We're good friends. Are you her mother?"

The woman pursed her lips and then said, "Young man, I'm afraid you've come to the wrong address. No one lives here by that name. It's only my husband and me. And we've been living here for years, so I know all our neighbors."

"But—"

"I'm so sorry," the woman said, and shut the door with a click. Her shadow faded from the door window.

Not knowing what to think, I walked back to the sidewalk and up to the corner. Once there, I looked back and studied the house. It told me nothing. My cell phone rang.

Mom's voice: "Where are you? Thought you'd be back by now."

"Couldn't find the right notebook," I said. "On my way."

When I got home, the first thing I did was check Jessica's address in the school directory. It read *1520 Lake Street*. That's where I had been.

I told myself that she might have moved since the directory was published last summer. Or that maybe the listing was a mistake, put in wrong, confused with another student.

Something explainable. Trouble was, she'd told me she *did* live on Lake Street.

I called Jessica's number. No answer. I left no message. She'd know I called.

I did get a text message from Lilly.

TLYK tx for coming to my party. Love the
H&M card. Will so wear what I get. Have a
great weekend. BBFN. XX L

Her message made me go over what I'd been told about Austin at the party. If he hadn't disappeared, as Jessica claimed, where was he? The kids had said Seattle. That gave me an idea. Since I had never given Lilly my cell phone number, she must have gotten it from the online school directory. On the first day I was at school, Batalie had given me the printed school directory from the beginning of the term, when Austin was enrolled.

I checked the Sevens page. Sure enough, his name was there, along with a phone number. Hopefully, it was a cell.

I texted:

Dear Austin Ganwell. My name is Tony
Gilbert. I am in the seventh grade at the

Penda School. I was able to get in because
you had to leave the school. I wanted to say
I'm sorry you had a bad time.
Tony Gilbert

I was not sure I would get an answer, but *any* answer
would be important. It would mean Austin had not disappeared, at least not the way Jessica said he had. I'd just have
to wait.

For the rest of the day I was with my folks searching for a
new couch, getting it delivered, giving away the old one—
all in a day. It took a lot of time. And I had forgotten my
phone.

When we returned home after dinner, there was a text
waiting for me.

dear tony gilbert. tks for text. glad u like
penda. Seattle pretty nice. say hi to all my
friends. tell them i'm ok. Austin Ganwell

In other words, what the kids at Lilly's party had told me
about Austin was true. What Jessica had told me about Austin was not.

What had Philip said? *Jessica is like, absolutely, totally . . . wacko with a capital* W.

In my head, I heard Ms. Foxton's words about Jessica: *I'm afraid truth is not one of her better character traits.*

I thought of calling Ms. Foxton, asking her about Austin. I had asked before, but she'd ducked it. Why?

Mom had given me her number. I searched my desk but couldn't find it. Anyway, I changed my mind. Me, calling the head of school. What could I say? Besides, Lilly's friends had asked me not to repeat what they told me about Austin.

It was about nine o'clock, and I was reading, when my cell phone rang.

"Hello?"

"You called?" It was Jessica.

Thinking fast, I said, "My parents were visiting some friends in your neighborhood, so I went to your Lake Street place, hoping you would be there."

"I just moved," she said.

"Didn't you tell me—"

"Dumb school didn't make a directory change. Better call first next time."

"Guess what? I just got a message—"

"See you," Jessica said, cutting me off. She didn't want to talk.

I was frustrated. Then, as I thought about it, I asked myself: *Why* hadn't she told me *where* she moved? I also remembered what the woman at the Lake Street house had said: *We've been living here for years, so I know all our neighbors.*

Except Jessica had told me she *did* live at that Lake Street address.

Maybe the Austin story Jessica told was fake, but I was certain the boy in the tower was *something* real. I decided I had to see him again, wanting to prove to myself that I *was* seeing him. That he was not in my head.

I figured out a way. For Sunday, my parents had planned a late-morning trip to the famous Muir Woods, just outside the city. We were to get a rental car and drive there. Before I took that trip with my parents, I'd go to school and look for the Penda Boy.

I set my alarm for seven thirty. Seven again.

Sunday, my alarm barely buzzed when I slapped it off and got out of bed. I dressed, slid keys into my pocket, and eased out of our apartment.

The day was chilly, breezy, the air ripe with the smell of the sea. Branches quivered, dropping fall's dead leaves, like a barber's clippings. To the east, the sun was just rising, sending out pink, red, and purple threads of light against the lowering clouds, the threads twisting into knots of color. Other than parked cars, the street was empty. Not one car moving. I did see a skinny man jogging with a lean dog on a long leash. A gray cat loped by. Overhead, a bird flapped its wings in slo-mo. I heard my own footsteps, or was it my beating heart?

Reaching the Penda School, I tried to recall where I'd stood that Sunday when I first saw the school. And the boy. Once there, I looked up.

The building—like the great tree by its side—was massive, dark, with quirky angles everywhere. In the early, low light, those irregular red walls were like shattered shadows. The entry-door glass glistened black as well. Higher windows were equally dark.

The ground trembled. *Earthquake*, I assumed, but I barely reacted, only thinking how ordinary they had become, like my acceptance of the Penda Boy. Though I believed *he* was a ghost, I had grown used to seeing him. But in some way I couldn't explain, I felt that the quakes and the boy were connected. Just as I was the only one who seemed to notice the quakes, I was the only one who saw the boy. And there I was, *wanting* to see him—whatever *he* was.

As I continued to stand in place, looking up, the school

was touched by sun devils—bars of sunlight piercing through the clouds. The weather vane—the angel Gabriel—seemed to tremble with life. From the top down, the rest of the tower was painted by the sun's rising glitter. Windows filled with molten gold. The school's redwood siding fairly glowed. It was as if the entire building was engulfed in fire.

Someone appeared behind the big tower's window. I was sure it was the Penda Boy. That he was looking at me. I wished I knew what he was thinking, if—whatever he was— he could think. *Does he really want my life? My soul? Where does Jessica fit in?*

Next second he was gone.

Seeing him removed all doubts. Although I knew the Penda Boy was not alive, I had seen him. He was there, a ghost. He had been staring at me as if trying to make a connection. But *what* did he want of me?

Wishing he would come back so I could see more, learn more, I remained on the street. He didn't return.

As time passed, I knew I had to get home before my parents woke and found me gone—which would mean explanations. I started off. At the first corner, the streetlight switched to red. No cars were coming, but out of habit I stopped. With no particular purpose, I turned and looked back at the school.

That was when I saw the school doors burst open. Out of the building came Jessica.

After momentary shock, my automatic reaction was to bob behind a parked car, but I poked my head up enough to see her hurry off the school steps, reach the sidewalk, and keep going. As always, she limped slightly, her long black hair swishing like a horse's tail. My first guess was that she was going to that address on Lake Street. At the first corner, however, she took a right turn and headed downhill. Wherever she was going, it was *not* toward Lake Street. I watched her go, wishing I could follow and see where she went. But I had to get back.

As I ran home, my mind fairly tumbled with questions. Why was Jessica in school early Sunday morning? Was she the one I had seen in the tower window? No, I was sure it had been the Penda Boy. My mind turned back to the first time I had seen the Penda School, that Sunday, when Uncle Charlie had appeared. Only then did I suddenly recall a girl looking out at me from the school's first floor. Had that been Jessica? Then, right after I saw her, I saw the Penda Boy in the high tower.

A horrifying thought jolted me: *What if they're together?*

I slipped back into our apartment, and my bed, so my

parents never knew I'd been out. I lay there, panting, thoughts jumbled, trying to untangle what I had seen. Again, were Jessica and the Penda Boy together? Who was my friend? Who was my enemy?

The truth was, I no longer knew.

That afternoon, my parents and I went to Muir Woods, a forest of gigantic, ancient redwoods. As always, Dad flung facts at me. For example: Some redwoods live for two thousand years. The average age of the trees is between five hundred and seven hundred years old. Certain redwood cones—not all—open up at extreme heat—like during a major forest fire. The seeds pop out only when they're needed. "If there is a crisis," said Dad, "old rules don't apply."

Maybe, since the Penda School was built of redwood, old rules didn't apply there either.

I used my cell phone to pull up a calendar. Halloween was in five days. Knowing that would be my crisis day, I felt Dad's words reverberate: *If there is a crisis, old rules don't apply.* What would be the new rules?

I reminded myself that the next day—Monday—I had an appointment to meet Bokor. He was supposed to give me information for my term paper.

Having become distrustful of everyone, I started to feel that Bokor—adviser to the Weird History Club—had pushed me into doing the paper about the Penda School. Was he giving me the plans because Jessica *wanted* him to, so that I—along with the Weird History Club—could catch the Penda Boy in a tower and destroy him before he got me? Those misgivings made me recall the class when Bokor spoke about ghosts, about Halloween. Did he do so because Jessica—and Mac— had *asked* questions about ghosts?

Even as I struggled for answers, new questions came up. For instance, I checked the earthquake listings for the day. There'd been lots of them, though absolutely *none* in San Francisco. But that morning I *had* felt one outside the Penda School. How could they only be *there*?

But the biggest question remained: Were Jessica and the ghost together, working to destroy me?

And Uncle Charlie's ghost. What if *he* too was with Jessica? That thought embarrassed me. There were lots of impossible things going on, but I refused to consider that one. In fact, I suddenly wished I hadn't banished him. *Uncle Charlie*, I thought, *why did you want me to come to Penda?*

Trouble was, I had told him to go away and had been successful. Why couldn't I make the rest of it go away?

Still, no matter where I looked, or what I asked, I had the feeling that I was being surrounded by things I didn't understand. Surrounded by an invisible army. Worse, there was no way to escape.

I slept badly. When I did get up Monday morning, I had to decide about the black tie. Jessica had said club rules required I wear something black each day. I put on the tie, worried that if I didn't, she would ask questions. I wanted to avoid that, having no desire to give her any idea about what I'd been told at the party.

In fact, when I got to Penda, the first person I met was Lilly. She rushed up.

"Tony, guess what?" she cried. "I got the cutest outfit at H&M with your card. A knit poncho, with a *great* collar, buttons, all in a pattern of pinks, reds, and purples. Matching purple leggings and a dark pink cap. Oh my God. So cute. Thank you." In her enthusiasm, she gave me a hug.

Embarrassed but pleased, I grinned, nodded, and said, "Nice." At the same time, I glanced up. Jessica was standing by the school doors looking down at us, her face full of contempt.

I went up the steps.

"What's up?" said Jessica.

"Not much," I said, wanting to get by her while trying to keep my face neutral. She grabbed my arm, surprising me with her strength. "You meeting with Bokor today?"

"Right after school."

"We don't have a lot of time."

"What do you mean?"

"Wake up, Tony," she said in an urgent whisper. "Halloween is in *four* days. If we're going to save you, we've got to get you into the towers. Get the Penda Boy. Before he gets you. You do understand, don't you?"

I nodded, mumbled, "Yeah," and stepped away, uneasy with her strength, her insistence. Most of all, I no longer believed her. *Keep away from her*, I told myself. It was what that Riley kid had said: *She's trouble.*

As I went up to the second floor, I looked for the Penda Boy. Not there. Only when I reached the top of the steps and looked back down did I see him below, gazing up at me.

He had said he wanted to talk to me. Okay, let him. I started toward him, but the next second he was engulfed by a mob of ascending students. When they cleared off, he was gone. Exasperated, I headed for class, telling myself that the next time he showed up, I would absolutely try to get him to talk.

When I walked into class, Batalie looked up. "Good morning, Tony."

"Morning," I returned, noticing he was wearing a black tie, which I hadn't seen on him before. Was he too a member of the Weird History Club?

I trusted no one.

It was a long day. Mostly, I waited for my meeting with Bokor. Though I didn't want to be there, I sat with the Weird History Club during recess. The cafeteria had been decorated for Halloween: black and orange twisted streamers, cutouts of jack-o'-lanterns, black cats with arched backs, cartoonlike ghosts, devils, and witches on broomsticks. There were a few tombstones with REST IN PEACE on them. As I looked about, it was as if the school was full of death. It seemed to make other people cheerful. Not me.

At the Weird History Club table, there was not much talk, except from Jessica.

She kept going on about what I should ask Bokor. The boys listened in silence, Mac biting his nails, Barney nibbling his sunflower seeds—so annoying—their eyes shifting from Jessica to me, like watchful cats. That made me think of what Mom had quoted: "The fog comes on little cat feet. It sits looking over harbor and city on silent haunches and then moves on."

Moves on where?

"The main thing," said Jessica, "is for you to find ways to get into the towers." When I realized she didn't say *we*, I excused myself by saying I had to be early for science.

During lunch, I sat with the kids who were at Lilly's party: so different from the Weird History Club. Babble and laughter about the party, the movie we saw. Even more excitement about the coming Halloween party and the costumes people were considering.

As before, Ian announced he was going to dress as the Penda Boy, which brought jeers from the other kids. "That's the night he disappeared," Ian protested. "It's a tradition. He *has* to be there."

As I headed back to class, Lilly was by my side.

"I wanted to say sorry about that Austin business," she whispered. "I think it upset you."

"It's okay," I said. "Anyway, I texted Austin."

"You did?"

"Yeah. He texted back to say hello to the class. That he was fine."

"That was so sweet of you." Lilly looked down at her shoes. "You going to tell Jessica what we told you?" she asked timidly.

"Wasn't planning to."

"I wish you wouldn't."

"Why?"

When she looked up, I saw fear in her eyes.

I said, "You're afraid of her, aren't you?"

She gave a tiny, embarrassed nod. Then she whispered, "She's . . . strange." Her eyes shifted to my black tie.

She must have realized I noticed her look, because she blushed. "Sorry. She's your friend," she said, and rushed away. I watched her weave through other kids. Among them was the Penda Boy, there, then gone.

No question: I was seeing him more often. He was becoming bolder. Was it because Halloween was closer? If the Penda Boy was after me—and I was sure he was—that would be his deadline too. *Dead-line*: the word made me wince.

Earlier, I had decided I would get the Penda Boy to talk to me. I turned away. I was sick of him. No, I was scared of him. For the rest of the day I took care not to be alone.

In the afternoon, I had history. A normal class, except that at the very end, as students were filing out, Bokor called, "Tony. We're meeting after school, right?"

I nodded, but reminded myself I should be careful what I said to him. *Trust no one.*

❖ ❖ ❖

School was over. As kids emptied homeroom, I looked up. Jessica was standing by the doorway, her black backpack slung over her shoulder. She gave me her pretty smile and a thumbs-up sign. I faked a smile back. As she went, I wondered, *Where does she live?*

I gathered the books I was supposed to read that night, stuffed them into my backpack, and headed out.

"Tony."

It was Batalie. Though the classroom was mostly empty, he beckoned me closer, as if needing to talk to me in private.

"I gather," he said in a low voice, his pink-rimmed eyes full of anxiety, "you heard about Austin at Lilly's birthday party."

"I suppose," I muttered, assuming one of the party kids had told him.

"May I ask you to keep it to yourself?"

"Sure," I said. He stepped closer to me, making me even more aware how old he was. He smelled of too much after-shave.

"The Penda School," he fairly hissed, "is a long-standing institution. Remember, 'Respect the past and protect the future.'"

"Protect who from what?" I blurted out. I never had gotten an answer to that question.

"So it may continue," he said with unexpected fierceness. "Have a good night, Tony. See you tomorrow."

"'Night," I said, wondering why he was so angry.

Bokor, sitting behind his desk, surrounded by papers and a few books, was waiting for me. In his baggy brown suit, he seemed enormous. He too was wearing a black tie.

"Tony, hello," he called in his big voice. "Glad you could come. Pull up a seat. Let me show you some wonderful stuff."

I sat down.

He started right off. "As I told you, for this term paper I'm interested in students developing an understanding of historical sources. Primary sources are original documents. Secondary sources are writings *about* the subject from a distance, so to speak. For example"—he slid a pile of paper toward me—"here's the *History of the Penda School*, which I wrote. Only a hundred pages. Go through it.

"I worked with letters, newspaper accounts, deeds, old school yearbooks, plus those old Penda student files in Ms. Foxton's office. Used Mrs. Penda's will too. All primary sources, listed in my bibliography. If you quote them directly, those are primary materials. Quote my *interpretation*, that's a secondary source. Make sense?"

"Think so."

He slid his book toward me. "Here's a copy for you."

"Thanks."

"Now this," he went on, lifting a roll of large papers, "is amazing."

He spread out the sheets, which were covered with what looked like webs of faint lines. "These are the original plans for the mansion that Mrs. Penda built back in 1884. As you might guess, with such an enormous building, and being so rich, Mrs. Penda had many servants. The servants lived in small bedrooms in the towers. In those days, servants were not to be seen. So—special stairways and rooms for servants. Most old mansions had back stairs, but here, they're inside the walls. For example"—he pointed to the plans—"here are steps that go from the old kitchen to the dining room. Over here, from Mrs. Penda's bedroom to her personal servant's quarters. And so on. It meant that those people, when summoned, could appear. Like magic." He laughed.

Like the Penda Boy, I thought.

"There was a system of bells to summon them. There's a story that only Mrs. Penda was allowed to ring them. Look," he went on, pointing to the plans, "from the room we're in now—once a guest bedroom—servant passages go directly to one of the smaller towers." He pointed across the classroom. "See that bookcase?"

I looked.

"Behind it is a door. The school is full of such doors. All sealed, of course."

"Does anyone use those old passages?" I asked.

"Not supposed to," he said with a smile. "But . . . it's fun to think about, isn't it?" he added.

No, I thought. "Sure," I said.

"Now, I can't give you these original plans, but I made copies. I'll just ask you not to share them with anyone. Can't have people sneaking around, can we? Agree?"

I nodded, realizing he had given me the *exact* information Jessica had asked me to get.

"There you go," he said. "You're on your way."

Where would that be? I asked myself.

Saying, "Thanks," I stuck the papers into my backpack. "Mr. Bokor," I blurted out, "you're a member of the Weird History Club, right?"

He lifted his tie. "Adviser," he said.

"In class, you said you believe in ghosts. Do you really? Do you think there are any in the towers?"

The playfulness in his face faded. He became older-looking, haggard, with a flash of fear.

"Do *I* believe in ghosts?" he repeated, as if trying to decide what answer to give. "Well, yes, some."

"Which ones?"

"Let's save that for another time." He turned away.

Dismissed, I thought, *Why won't he say more? The whole school is on edge. As if everyone has a deadline.*

That night, sitting at my desk, I studied the Penda mansion plans. I could see where the secret stairways and servants' rooms were within the building's walls. Made me think of Swiss cheese, full of hidden holes.

Did the Penda Boy live in one of those servants' rooms? Did he use the old passages? Go through old doors? Or maybe he didn't need doors. Bokor had mentioned that servants were summoned by a jangling bell that only Mrs. Penda was allowed to ring. Who summoned the Penda Boy? Jessica?

When my phone rang, I jumped.

"Hello?"

"Hey, Jessica."

Hearing her made me tense. Even so, I wished I knew from where she was calling.

She said, "What did Bokor tell you?"

"Lots of stuff," I said evasively.

"About the servants' doors and stairs? Servants' rooms? Did he give you plans?"

"Yeah," I said.

She said, "Bring them to school tomorrow." It came out like an order. Before I could say anything, she hung up. Her calls were quick. As if she was afraid I'd somehow track her.

I kept thinking how insistent she was about my getting rid of the Penda Boy. Why did she never say *how* I was going to do it? I was beginning to worry the Weird History Club was trying to deliver me to him.

I started to read Bokor's *History of the Penda School*. It began with information about Mrs. Penda and her husband. How when he died, Mrs. Penda inherited a redwood forest company. Then she died, and shortly afterward her boy died. It was Mrs. Penda's will that created the school.

I paused and reread the line:

Mrs. Penda died, and shortly afterward, her boy died.

That seemed wrong. Wasn't it the other way around? Hadn't the Penda Boy died *first*? Wasn't *that* how the school began? Didn't Mrs. Penda set the school up in his *memory*?

On that first Sunday, when we stood outside the school, Dad had read the school brochure to me. I was sure it had said Mrs. Penda had died from grief *after* her son died. On my first day in school, Ms. Foxton had said the same thing.

I went to where my parents were watching the news.

"Dad," I said, "remember how you read the Penda School brochure they sent us? Do we still have it?"

"No idea. We've thrown out so much stuff."

"I need it for a history paper I'm writing about the school."

Mom said, "I think there was a bunch on display in the school office. I bet you could get one there."

In my room, on a piece of paper, I copied Bokor's sentences.

Mrs. Penda died, and shortly afterward, her son died.
Her will established the school.

Something was not right.

Next morning, needing to think things out, but tired of Jessica telling me what to do, I decided to leave the plans at home. Even so, Jessica was waiting for me on the school steps. The first thing she said was, "Did you bring the plans?"

I said, "Forgot them."

Her look turned angry, upset. "You live close. Get them during lunchtime."

Determined to stand up to her, I said, "Only Eights are

allowed off campus during lunch."

"Wimp. I'll walk you home after school."

"I have to stay."

"Why?" she snapped.

"Our history paper is due. I started late. Need to check some dates in the library."

She backed down, but for the first time, I saw fright in *her* eyes.

With her voice more under control, she said, "Just make certain you bring them tomorrow for the club meeting."

I was sure she wanted to be forceful, but I heard anxiety too. She had not shown fear before. Why would *she* be frightened now?

She answered my unspoken question when she added, "Tony, you're running out of time."

Thoughts flashed through my mind. *Is it me she's worried about? The Penda Boy?* And for the first time I had this thought: *Or is she worried for herself?*

Why would she be?

At three school was over and most of the students left the building. After watching to make sure Jessica had gone too, I went to the school office. Mrs. Z was at her desk. On her jacket collar was a silk flower, black.

Black was the new happy.

"Hello, Tony," she said, friendly enough. "How are you? What brings you here?"

"I'm writing a paper about the history of the school."

"Oh, fun."

"I was thinking, do you have anything that would help me?"

"Oh dear. I don't believe I do. Have you spoken to Mr. Bokor? He's our local historian."

"He gave me some stuff."

"Actually," she said, "the material we have is in Ms. Foxton's office. I guess you could call it an archive. Info on all former students. That sort of thing. Unfortunately, she's at an out-of-school meeting. She should be back soon. In the meantime, why don't you take a look at those old yearbooks?" She pointed to the table by the couch. "With names and pictures, year by year, of everyone who ever went here. The way people dressed . . . so interesting. Make yourself comfortable."

"Thanks," I said. "Can I take one of these school brochures?"

"Help yourself."

I glanced at the painting of Mrs. Penda. As I looked at the woman's angry face, I was reminded of the way Jessica had looked when I'd told her I hadn't brought Bokor's plans.

I dropped my backpack to one side of the couch and flipped through the pages of a brochure. On the second page, I came upon:

A Brief History of the Penda School

The passage I was looking for was right up front.

The Penda School came into existence in 1897, when Mrs. Penda, a wealthy widow who owned redwood forests in Northern California, established the school soon after her only child, a boy, died. So great was her grief that shortly afterward she too passed away. All the same, she left her mansion and an endowment for a boys' and girls' school that they might "Respect the past and protect the future."

I took out the paper on which I'd copied what Bokor had written in his history of the school.

Mrs. Penda died, and shortly afterward, her son died. Her will established the school.

The two statements did not agree. Did the boy die before or after his mother died? Did it matter?

I studied the painting of the Penda Boy. His eyes full of fear. Pleading. What was he trying to say?

"Tony."

I looked up. Mrs. Z was standing over me. "Will you be staying long?" she asked.

"About to look at the yearbooks."

"That's fine. I have to speak to one of the janitors. I'll be right back. Ms. Foxton should return soon."

"I'm okay."

She left the room.

I put down the brochure and plucked out the earliest yearbook, 1898. It was a real book, cloth-covered, heavy, the date stamped in gold. I opened it. The pale yellow paper was thick with a slight sheen. On the first page was this statement:

The Penda School has come into existence because of the death of Mrs. Reese Penda. Shortly after her adopted son died, she died, and according to the terms of Mrs. Penda's will, the school was established.

There it was again: the boy died *before* Mrs. Penda died. And something else was different: the Penda Boy was an *adopted* son. Did *that* matter? Over the years, facts seem to have been changed.

On the next page was a list of school officers. Then came a page of faculty names. What followed were group photos of each class, starting with the first grade and continuing to the eighth.

Under the picture of "Our First Seventh Grade," boys and girls were listed separately. In the girls' list I saw

Jessica Richards

Not believing what I was seeing, I read the name over and over. I studied the faces in the image. The pictures were small, like faded memories. Two girls with dark hair looked like Jessica might have looked. Except obviously it could *not* be her.

I pulled out another yearbook, the one for 1905. On the first page was a class picture:

Our Seventh Grade

I read the girls' names. Among them was

Jessica Richards

Jessica had told me her family had always been in the school. Did they all have the same name? Not likely. More and more puzzled, I pulled out another year, 1920, and flipped through the book until I came to the first-grade class. Sure enough, among the names was

Jessica Richards

It made no sense.

I turned to another yearbook.

Jessica Richards

Why did her name keep reappearing? How could she have been a student for more than a hundred years? Impossible.

As I stared at the name, I remembered my first day at Penda, when we'd met with Ms. Foxton in her office. She had held up a manila folder and said, "Since 1897, we've kept track of every student," and she had glanced toward the file cabinets.

I thought, *Then there should be records for every Jessica Richards*. If I checked the files, I might make sense of what I had discovered. Hadn't Ms. Foxton said, "If you can think of any way I can be helpful, my door is always open"?

I looked toward Ms. Foxton's office. The door *was* partly open. A light was on.

I crossed over to the school office door and peeked out into the reception hall. The chandelier was swaying slightly, causing the glass bits to tinkle softly. There was no sign of Mrs. Z.

I stood before Ms. Foxton's office, trying to decide if I should go in or not. Though I knew that Mrs. Z was around and that Ms. Foxton would be returning soon, I felt I *had* to learn more. *Had to.* That's my explanation for why—though I knew I'd be in huge trouble if discovered—I stepped into Ms. Foxton's office.

No one was there, but the room looked exactly the way it did whenever I had to speak to Ms. Foxton: The large desk with three chairs before it. Behind the desk that photograph of joyful kids; on the right wall, the fake-looking fireplace; on the wall opposite, the wooden file cabinets; standing on one of the files, a plastic flashlight; on the wall next to the door, the large wooden chest. Nothing had changed.

Shutting the door behind me softly, trying to move as fast as I could, I went right to the first of the cabinets, the one with brass letters that read *1897*. The drawer slid out noiselessly, revealing row upon row of file folders with tabs sticking up, each with a student's name, last name first, all neatly written—like gravestones, I thought, and was reminded of the cemetery where Uncle Charlie was buried.

I grabbed the flashlight, turned it on, so I could see the files better. My fingers flicked over the names, front to back. *Culley, Jacob. Kimball, Timothy. Potter, Elisa.* And so on. But no *Richards, Jessica.*

I pulled out the 1912 files. *Abel, Miller, Tagent.* So on. No *Richards, Jessica.*

I kept going fast, cabinet after cabinet, year after year, name after name. No Jessica Richards. Not even Richards. Or Jessica. Baffled, I finally drew out this year's files. *Budson. Minks. Pallister. Smathers.* Even my name, *Gilbert, Anthony,* was there.

Everybody but Jessica Richards.

I closed the last file and tried to make sense of what I had *not* found. Ms. Foxton had said there was a file for *every* student. How could Jessica's name appear in *all* those yearbooks but not be in *any* of the school files?

I was still there, flashlight in hand, trying to figure things out, when I heard the sounds of someone moving about in the front office. My stomach lurched. Mrs. Z—or Ms. Foxton—had come back.

❖ ❖ ❖

It took no thought to know that if I was discovered in Ms. Foxton's office it would be a disaster. For a nanosecond, I considered staying where I was, at least until Mrs. Z left. She would have to go sometime. Then I realized it could be an hour or more before she went. Or she might step into the office to turn out lights or leave papers—and find me. Or it might be Ms. Foxton and she might come in.

I had to get out of the office.

I couldn't go out the way I'd come in. I'd be seen. My next notion was to hide under the desk. But being discovered there would be just as bad.

Panic growing, I went over to the fireplace, thinking I could crawl up into the chimney. On hands and knees, I peered in, and up. The way was blocked. In other words, it was fake, just as I'd thought when I first saw it.

I considered the fancy wooden chest. I was sure it too was fake—that is, empty, except maybe it just held a few envelopes and folders. If it was mostly empty, it was big enough to hold me. Though it was coffin-like, it wouldn't kill me to lie there for an hour or two.

More noise came from the front office, pushing me to try the chest. Only trouble: when I put my hand to the edge of the lid and pulled up, once, twice, it would not give.

Desperate, I scooted back to Ms. Foxton's desk, snatched up the letter-opening knife, and stuck it under the chest lid. With a *pop*, the lid opened. I dropped the knife to the floor, grasped the lid with two hands, lifted, and looked inside.

Going down into darkness were steps.

I stared, not certain if the steps were actually there or something I was imagining. But the more I gawked, the more certain I was that they were real.

I was still looking when new sounds came from the front office. Knowing that at any moment someone might come in and find me, I looked around the office, snatched up the flashlight, and pointed its pathetic beam along the steps. What I saw were old wooden steps, worn in the middle, as if used over a long period. Aiming the light deeper, I saw that the steps led down to some kind of space.

Wanting only not to be discovered, I gripped the flashlight, stepped into the chest, and went down a few steps. Once a bit below, I reached over my head and tried—as gently as possible—to ease the lid down. Jittery, I miscalculated. The lid dropped with a loud bang.

Scared that I might have been heard, I crouched down and clicked off the flashlight. Heart racing, I held my breath and listened.

I heard footsteps cross Ms. Foxton's office, in and then out. I imagined Mrs. Z checking the room, finding no one, then—hopefully—leaving for the day. Though I allowed myself a breath of relief, I made myself count to three hundred. And then some.

Feeling safer, I reached up and pushed against the lid. It wouldn't give. I pushed harder. No success. I tried again. When it still wouldn't budge, my heart sank. The force of the dropping lid must have caused it to stick shut. I was not going to get out the way I came in.

Sitting on the steps in the dark, I tried to figure out what to do. I flicked on the flashlight. The feeble yellow beam revealed a bottom step and wood flooring, nothing else. Even so, that seemed the only way out. Not really wanting to go down, I made another try at the overhead lid. It refused to move.

I reexamined the wooden steps. They were steep, barely three feet wide, with rough, splintery wooden walls crowding in from either side. I had no more idea what was below than when I had first looked. The only thing clear was that I didn't have much choice other than to go down.

Trying to steady myself so as not to fall, I held the flashlight in my left hand and then pressed my right hand against a wall. I began to descend like a little kid, moving one step at a time, feeling my way with my feet. When I reached the bottom, I played the flashlight beam about, wanting to see where I was. It was a small room. The air was clammy and smelled musty. The walls were thin wood slats, dry and unfinished, in some cases warped. Here and there, rusty square-headed nails stuck out like blunted spikes. The sagging ceiling was wood too. On the wooden floor lay random piles of clothing. The only sound I heard was the rasping saw of my own nervous breathing.

Across the room, opposite where I stood, was a closed door; against the right wall, an old bed with a rust-corroded frame, its feet shaped like clutching claws; on the bed, a thin mattress, plus a jumble of blankets. The blankets were torn in some places, frayed at the edges. At the bed's head was a lumpy gray pillow. It was indented—the indentation darker than the surrounding area—suggesting a head had rested there.

On the left wall was what looked like a freestanding closet, its two doors partly open. I aimed my light inside. On the bottom lay more clothing. Stepping closer, I saw what appeared to be a shirt, socks, and a skirt. Amid the clothing lay a pair of black sneakers with red shoelaces. By the closet was a rickety wooden chair from which a black backpack hung.

The way the clothing was scattered gave the impression

that, though the room was old, it had been occupied recently. Someone, it seemed, had slept in the bed. But who, I asked myself, would live in such a place? A janitor? Was it a servant's room, abandoned years ago? It was right under Ms. Foxton's office. Did *she* use this place? I could make no connection between her—well dressed, neat, and proper—and this disorderly, decaying room.

I peered back into the closet and considered the clothing: white collared blouses, pleated blue skirts. The standard dress of Penda girls. Then it struck me: the black sneakers with red shoelaces were like the ones I'd seen Jessica wear.

Next second I recalled seeing her coming out of the building Sunday morning. And that she didn't live at that Lake Street address, which was in the school directory.

Could this be where Jessica lived?

I considered the black backpack hanging from the chair. It looked like Jessica's. When I lifted it from its place and hefted it, it seemed as if something was inside.

Unfastening the clasp and using the flashlight, I peered in. There were papers and a few books. I pulled out a sheet. In a glance, I saw penciled geometry problems. On the top of the page, a name had been written:

Jessica Richards

I stared at the name, returned the paper to the backpack, fished around, and pulled out a paperback book. It was a copy of *The Old Man and the Sea*. On the inside of the cover was a name.

Jessica Richards

I felt around and found something else: her pale blue tube of moisturizer. It *was* Jessica's room. Where she lived. Her talk of her father, mother: fake. But . . . *why* would she live here? Alone?

In search of more clues, I went back to *The Old Man and the Sea*. On the inside back cover, in the same handwriting as before, another name was written.

Anthony Gilbert

My name. Circled. Next to the circle, the words *STINKS OF DEATH* had been written in block letters. There was a line, an arrow, pointing from those words about death to my name.

And the number seven, written seven times.

Below that were the words *Let the dead bury the dead.*

I had no time to figure out a meaning. I kept thinking that if this was Jessica's room—and I was sure it was—what would happen if she came back and found me?

At the thought, fright surged through me. My heart pounded. All I knew was that I had to get away, fast.

I hurried back up the steps and used my shoulder to press against the chest lid, so hard it hurt. It still refused to open. Knowing I was trapped, I flicked off the light and sat on a step. I felt claustrophobic. The stale smell of the air sickened me. I felt woozy.

Trying to contain my mounting fright, I crept back down. Flashlight in hand, I pointed the beam around the room. The light flickered and faded, as if about to die. I shook it. It strengthened. As far as I could see, there appeared to be only one way out: the door on the opposite wall.

I crossed the room, put my hand to the knob, turned it, and pushed. The door opened onto a narrow hallway. My flashlight revealed floor, ceiling, and walls of old wood, like the room in which I'd just been. But what lay before me was only darkness.

Feeling I had no choice, I went forward.

I shut the door behind me and began to walk. I had taken no more than six steps before I told myself not to leave that door shut, fearful that it might remain closed the way the chest lid had. I darted back, grabbed the doorknob with all my strength and pulled, only to have the knob come off in my hand. Trying to swallow down my shock, I just stood there, doorknob in hand.

Not wanting to leave any evidence of my presence, I put the knob shaft back into the square hole. Then I used the faltering flashlight beam to see a few feet ahead.

I crept along the hallway, moving cautiously. Nothing on the floor to impede me. Nothing on the walls to suggest where I was. But also nothing to tell me where I was heading.

I continued on, noticing an old bell hanging from the ceiling. I put a finger to it, causing it to tinkle in a tinny, metallic way, its little sound making me feel even more alone.

A few steps farther on, I came upon a short hall leading to the right. At its end was another door, latched. Hoping the door might lead to a way out, I went to it, unfastened the latch, and looked in.

It was a room smaller than the one in which I'd just been. Four chairs sat about a round table, as if placed for a meeting. Other chairs stood against the walls. In the center of the table stood a partly burned candle, its wick short and bent like a charred, crooked finger. Around the candle's base lay a gray crust of hard wax.

Unfortunately, the only door was the one I'd used to enter.

My first thought was that the room was a place where—in times past—servants met, or ate. Then I caught a faint whiff of burning, as if the candle had been recently lit. On the floor, I noticed a small mound of sunflower husks, as Barney might have left. That made no sense to me. Why would *he* have been here?

Retreating, I shut the door, latched it, and returned to the hall and continued in the same direction I had been going.

I reached a dead end, a wooden wall of horizontal slats, with what appeared to be plaster that had oozed between the slats before hardening. It took a few seconds of looking about to realize that against the wall was a rusty metal spiral stairway. When I pointed the flashlight up, all I could determine was that the steps rose up into darkness, with not so much as a flicker of light to suggest where or how high they reached.

Recalling the concealed rooms and walls in the building, I decided that all of this was where, in olden days, servants came and went: the hidden passages. There had to be a way out. Determined to find it, I reached for the iron railing. Though the metal was icy cold, I gripped it and began to climb.

Pointing the unreliable flashlight beam up, keeping my head tilted back, hoping to see where I was going, I climbed steadily, if slowly, moving in tight circles, tight enough that I became woozy.

I didn't know how far I had climbed when I reached a place with a small landing off to one side. Dimly, I could see a door set into the wall, as well as another dangling bell. I imagined it was the sealed door that Jessica had shown me on the second floor of the school. I tried the doorknob. It wouldn't turn. Even when I gave the door a hard push, it remained shut. Sealed.

I returned to the steps, looked up, and saw nothing but more blackness. I looked down. It was just as shadowy. I chose to go up. But as I swung back around, my flashlight hit the banister and popped out of my hand. I lunged for it but missed. It dropped like a noisy falling star, *bump, bump, bump,* until sounds and light ceased altogether. Afraid to move, I remained where I was, surrounded by absolute and silent darkness.

I'm not sure how long I stood there, only knowing I had little choice but to continue. Clinging tightly to the banister, staring into blackness, I forced myself to go up again.

Round and round I went, pulling as much as climbing. In all that blackness, I had no idea if I passed other landings, or other doors. I just kept going. I did sense I was moving up into one of the building's towers, perhaps the tallest one.

I wasn't sure how far I'd gone—I was trembling with cold, and tension, and had lost all sense of time and space—when I realized that the darkness above me had begun to thin, to lighten, just enough to see that I was approaching a ceiling. Moreover, the ceiling had an opening. The spiral steps were coming to an end.

Desperate to get free, I scampered up the remaining steps and poked my head up into a small, dim room. It stank of mildew, mold, and decay. Across the room, opposite where I poked up my head, was a dust-clotted window, through which seeped some shrouded light.

I went higher, pulling myself into the room. At first, the room appeared to be empty. Only as my eyes adjusted to the dimness did I realize that on the room's far side was a small, low bed. On the bed, back toward me, lay someone. Thinking I had come upon Jessica, my heart lurched.

The person sat up. It was the Penda Boy.

The Penda Boy had died more than a hundred years ago, but as far as I could see, he might just as well have stepped right out of the painting in the school office. True, his clothing was much more faded and tattered than in the painting, but I had no doubt it was he.

If he was a ghost—and I believed he was—there was nothing ghostlike about him. Nothing frightening. Not like some fake movie or TV ghost. I could not see through him. His eyes, which were blue, didn't gleam or appear wicked. The only unusual thing about him was a faint glow that seemed to come from within, a glimmering like what comes from a see-in-the-dark wristwatch. What I saw, mostly, was a sad boy in cast-off clothing and odd shoes who made me think of a homeless child.

We stood staring at each other until he said, "You've been avoiding me." He had a small boy's voice, impatient, with a hint of whining.

"Are you . . . are you Mrs. Penda's son?"

"Not a bit," he said, his voice abruptly turning defiant.

"Who . . . who are you, then?"

"The boy she claimed as her son."

"What do you mean?"

"Mrs. Penda wanted people to believe I was her child. I have no idea what my real name is. She gathered me up from Market Street and put me in the school to use me."

"Use you?"

"To keep herself alive."

"How . . . how could she do that?"

"She took most of my soul so she could live."

"Are you . . . dead, then?"

"Somewhere between dead and alive."

"Is she . . . alive?"

"The same."

"But . . . where is she?"

"Below."

"Here?" I said. "In the school?"

"Where else would she be? This building is nothing more than a home for her. A school of the dead. A monument to her wickedness."

When I just stared at him, he went on. "I was the first soul she tried to take. Back then, she didn't do it very well, which is why part of me didn't die."

"Does she know you're here?"

"Of course. She has tried to get rid of me many times, but I always get away. You may be certain I've worked very hard to make sure she doesn't see me, though once, we scuffled and I broke her leg. There isn't that much life in me. The energy I have allows only one person to see me. I usually pick the one she's chosen. Like you."

"What do you mean, 'chosen'?"

"Do you think," he said with scorn, "that this school exists for students? Don't be stupid. It's here so Mrs. Penda can take young souls. She does it every seven years. The soul she takes renews her life, and a few friends' lives. She's done so for more than a hundred years. What do you think that school slogan means? 'Respect the past and protect the future.' Respect *Mrs. Penda*. Protect *Mrs. Penda*."

"But why me?"

"You were close to someone who died. Whoever it was, a part of you died too. I smell it on you. It's very obvious. I'm sure Mrs. Penda smelled it too. It's harder for her to take the soul of a fully alive person. Easier to take someone half dead, the way you are."

"How . . . how will they take my soul?"

"They'll get you into one of the towers and draw out your soul. Bokor knows how. Painful—to be sure—but they don't care."

"You said Mr. Bokor . . . are there more?"

"Bokor taught Mrs. Penda his arts. Then there's Mr. Batalie. And his wife, the woman they call Mrs. Z."

"Batalie's *wife*?"

The boy nodded. "She stands guard over the whole school. And," he added, "they have their servants."

"Servants?"

"A few children—previously taken—who do what they are told."

Mac, Barney, and Jessica, I thought, and then asked, "What happens to the others?"

"They wander about searching for souls so they can live again. It's you they want now. If they don't get your soul, they'll perish. In fact, the whole building will go. It's preserved solely by the force of Mrs. Penda's being."

I suddenly understood the fear I kept seeing in *their* eyes. It was not *me* about whom they were worried, but *their* own existence.

"What happens if they . . . take my soul?"

"You become a wandering ghost, or perhaps a servant to Mrs. Penda—and her friends—while she becomes young and starts school again for seven more years. She's done it many times. If you're going to save yourself, you need to listen to me. You have very little time. Three days! Tell me what the old woman asked you to do."

"I don't know any old woman."

"Oh, don't be a pudding head!" he cried, his voice shrilling with exasperation. "Mrs. Penda disguises herself as someone young. Black hair and, with her vanity, looking older than her classmates."

"*Jessica?*" I said.

"Exactly."

I stared at him. In the momentary silence he said, "There's someone else seeking you."

"Who?"

"I'm not sure. One of Mrs. Penda's victims, I think. A former student. He's often around, looking to come back to life. An older man."

"What does he look like?"

"Gray hair flops over his forehead. Dressed in a checkered shirt. Tan suspenders."

"That's Uncle Charlie! Have you seen him?"

"I don't know who he is, but I've been seeing him often lately."

"But if you saw—"

He cut me off. "Listen to me. I don't care about the ones already lost. I'm trying to stop them from getting new ones. But we don't have much time. Tell me what Mrs. Penda asked you to do."

"During the Halloween party they intend to open one of the sealed doors so I can get into the towers. Since I'm the only one who sees you, I'm to lead them to you so they can get rid of you. But . . . they haven't told me how."

He said, "Yes, she wants to get rid of me. But only you can lead her to me. It's your soul she needs. Very well. Do as she tells you. Which door will you go through?"

"I don't know."

"Find out and let me know. As soon as you pass through,

I'll be there. I'll hide you from them until Halloween at midnight. If we can keep you alive until then, they'll come to an end.

"Now, will you," he asked, reverting to that sad look I had seen so often, "help me?"

"I have to ask you about the old man who—" Suddenly bells began to ring.

"What's that?" I said, startled.

"Mrs. Penda is summoning her friends to a meeting. Her 'board of trustees,' she calls them."

"Where do they meet?"

"At the bottom."

I thought of the meeting room. "Will they come up here?"

"Do they know you are in the building?"

"I'm not sure. Please, you have to get me out."

"Are you going to help me or not? The last one promised to help but ran away."

"Austin?"

"I believe that was his name. He lacked courage."

I turned back toward the steps.

"Stop! You can't get away without me. You need my help. I need yours. We must come to an agreement."

"I just want to get out of here."

"And I don't want them to remain the way they are,

pretending to care for children when they only mean to use them. I'm tired of being on guard all the time, tired of trying to save the one they pick. Over the years, I've lost too many. You're the best chance I have to stop them. It's so close to their deadline. If you help me, we can destroy them."

"Will you really protect me?"

"If we agree."

I looked toward the steps and then back to him. He had come closer and was holding out his hand. I didn't know what else to do, but I reached out. It was like shaking hands with water.

"Follow me," he said, and went to the head of the steps.

I hesitated.

"You'll be able to see," he assured me. He started down. Sure enough, the soft glow that emanated from within him was enough to show me where to place my feet.

Down we went, round and round. How far it was, I didn't know, but he led me to a little landing like the one I'd found before. A door was embedded in the wall. He lifted his hand as if about to push it open.

"Can I ask you something?"

"Be quick," he whispered.

"That old man you saw—"

"A ghost. One of Mrs. Penda's friends."

"Are you sure of that?"

"Of course I am. Now go."

"How," I asked, "are we to talk again?"

"I'll think of a way."

That he used the same words as Jessica made me suddenly suspicious. At the same moment, he put his small hand to the door. It swung open noiselessly. Stepping to one side, he said, "Hurry."

No need to be urged. I hurried through the doorway and found myself in a deserted classroom, where a window allowed in some dwindling daylight. I looked back. The boy had gone. The door was nothing but the faintest of outlines on the wall.

I all but tumbled down the steps to the reception hall. Seeing that the school office door was open and lights were on—suggesting people were there—I raced out through the main doors.

Once on the sidewalk, I started for home, but, unable to keep from looking back, I stopped. My eyes went to the high tower window. I was sure I saw the Penda Boy looking down.

I tore home as if my life depended on it.

Which I thought it did.

At home—my parents had not yet come from work—I slammed the door to my room, threw myself on my bed, and pressed a pillow over my eyes. No need to see. My head burst with images, from the time I discovered the steps within the chest to when the Penda Boy let me out into that empty classroom.

He had said lots of appalling things, but nothing worse than about Uncle Charlie. Some of the things Uncle Charlie had said came back to me, such as, "Hey, Tony, wouldn't it be great if the two of us never died?" and "When I go, I really want you to join me."

I could have no doubts: Uncle Charlie had arranged for me to come to Penda so I might enter Mrs. Penda's seven-year cycle, so he could come back to life. That's why I'd seen him when I first came to the school. That's how people like Batalie knew I was his relative. That's how Jessica knew where I lived. *He'd* told them.

I scolded myself: Uncle Charlie would not, could not do that to me. It was too awful. Let him be a ghost, but not one plotting to kill me. I refused to believe it.

Pushing those thoughts away, I went over the agreement I'd made with the Penda boy: that I would pretend to go along with Jessica. Instead of leading her to the boy, he would hide me—in one of the towers, I supposed—until midnight on Halloween. According to him, that would be the end of Mrs. Penda and the school, whatever that meant.

But . . . I had heard so many lies I had to ask myself if what the Penda Boy had said was true. In the end, I decided I needed to prove to myself that Jessica *was* Mrs. Penda. It would have to wait until tomorrow.

At dinner that evening, Mom said, "How was school today?"

"Fine."

Dad said, "Same old, same old?"

"Mostly," I replied, eyes on my spaghetti and meatballs.

Then he asked, "Your school do anything special for Halloween?"

I looked up. "They have a big party. And . . . I need a costume."

Dad asked, "What are you thinking of being?"

"Alive."

Mom said, "That's not very funny."

It was not meant to be.

That night I should have worked on my history paper. Instead, I walked my slackline. Or tried to. Unable to concentrate, I kept falling. When my cell phone rang, I knew it would be Jessica. I considered not answering but decided that wouldn't be smart. No point in letting her sense anything of what I'd learned.

"Hello."

"Hey, it's Jessica. Tomorrow, Weird History Club. Last meeting before Halloween. Have you been studying the school plans?"

"Yes," I lied.

"Learn them. But bring them to school." There was more tension in her voice than before.

I asked, "Is Bokor going to be there?"

"Why do you need to know?"

"He said not to share the plans."

She was silent a moment. Then she said, "Bring them. I'll take care of him."

"Okay," I said with a new understanding of what she meant.

"Tony . . ."

"What?"

"I'm your friend," she said. "I'm trying to save you."

"Sure."

"We don't want to run out of time."

She was right, for both of us.

Why, I puzzled, was Jessica so insistent that I study the plans? If she *was* Mrs. Penda, she had to be familiar with every secret passage and room in the building.

To calm down, I decided I would work on the history paper. Usually I dropped my backpack by the door when I came in, but when I looked, it wasn't there. I searched. It wasn't in the apartment.

Then I remembered: I had left it in the school office. Which meant Ms. Foxton would know I'd been there. I could only hope she wouldn't notice it.

I went into my parents' room to say good night. Mom was in bed, reading. Dad was at his desk.

"Going to sleep," I announced.

"'Night," my parents chorused.

I turned to go.

"Oh, Tony," my mother called. "I'm sorry. I forgot. Late this afternoon in the middle of a busy meeting, I got a call from Ms. Foxton."

I froze. "About what?"

"I guess you left your backpack in the school office. She wanted you to know she found it. Asked if you got home, though why she should ask that, I can't imagine. I assured her you did." She smiled. "Not that I really knew."

I sat at my desk, trying to make sense of Ms. Foxton's call. She must have seen the backpack. Why would she call Mom about it and ask if I got home? Was that her way of saying she knew I was in her office? Did she know I went down the steps?

I remembered Ms. Foxton's letter opener, which I'd used to pry open the chest lid. I had left it on the floor. Had she found that too?

I put the building plans in an envelope and went to bed, but all I could think about was what, if anything, Ms. Foxton knew. I wished I had asked the Penda Boy if *she* was working with Jessica.

Did I have *any* friends at the school?

I was having nightmares even before I slept.

In the morning, I went to school reluctantly, the manila envelope of plans in my hand. My black tie—like a noose—hung loosely around my neck. The gray, misty air reminded me of that foggy day when I felt Uncle Charlie's hands on my arm. As my eyes tried to focus on the blurry world, I told myself I had to be friendly with Jessica so she wouldn't guess what I had discovered. But how do you act friendly to someone when you know she is planning to kill you?

She was waiting for me at the school door, a stern look on her face. "Did you bring the plans?" she demanded.

"Sure," I said, trying to sound easy.

"Where are they?"

I held up the envelope.

She rewarded me with a smile. "Knew I could count on you," she said, which only added to my discomfort.

We walked into school together, but I halted by the office. "Have to go in for a minute," I said.

Jessica said, "I'll wait."

I didn't like that, but I had no choice.

Mrs. Z, behind her desk, looked up and smiled. On her desk was the red flashlight.

Seeing it stopped me cold. The last I'd seen it was when I dropped it from the spiral steps. In other words, *someone* had found it at the bottom. Put it on the desk.

"Good morning, Tony," said Mrs. Z. "Your backpack is right over there."

She knew about it too.

"Thanks," I muttered, grabbed it and headed out. My head was whirling. If someone knew about my backpack, the letter opener, *and* the flashlight—and connected the dots—they knew where I had gone. The most obvious choice was Mrs. Z—Batalie's wife, the school watchdog. But she hadn't acted any differently toward me. I went back to worrying about the call my mom had received from Ms. Foxton. Was Ms. Foxton on my side, or Mrs. Penda's?

When I came out of the office, Jessica was waiting for me. I checked her face for some hint that she knew anything. I saw no sign, though she did say, "How come your backpack was in there?"

I managed a shrug. "Left it at school last night when I went home. Somebody found it. Called my mother."

She said nothing. We went up the steps side by side. "Is Lilly your girlfriend?" she suddenly said.

"We're just friends," I said. "Why you asking?"

Giving me one of her great smiles, she said, "Just making sure I'm still your best friend."

The words felt like a punch in the stomach.

"Tell you what," she said. "Better give those plans to me. I'll go over them during recess and lunch. By the time we have our regular meeting this afternoon, I'll have worked things out."

I handed over the envelope.

As we went up, I looked over to the other staircase. For just a moment, the Penda Boy was there, eyes on me. I had no doubt he was reminding me of my promise: that I would go along with Jessica on Halloween. I glanced at her, relieved she couldn't see him.

We got to the second floor. She said, "Have to go talk to

Bokor. Remind him of our last meeting."

Would she tell him I gave her the plans?

I walked into class. Batalie was at his desk. He looked up at me, fear in his eyes. I understood his fear now.

"Tony," Lilly called out in her cheerful way, gesturing for me to sit near her. Her total lack of knowing was a relief. I sat down next to her.

She said, "Lunchtime, a bunch of us are going to work on plans for Halloween. Games and stuff. You should come."

"Sure."

"Do you know what you're going to be yet?"

"Nope. You?"

She grinned. "I've got a great idea."

"What?"

"Not telling. It's so much more fun when people don't know who you are. Did anyone tell you there's a contest for the best costume?"

I said, "How come the school makes such a big thing about Halloween?"

"I suppose because of the Penda Boy."

"What do you mean?"

"You know, people always say his ghost is in one of our towers. That he died on a Halloween night. So it's as if we're having a birthday party to remember him. Oh my God, a school for the dead. Don't you love it?"

Jessica came into the room. Her eyes went right to Lilly and me. She didn't say a word, just smirked.

When classes began, I couldn't pay attention. At recess, I stayed put, doing homework I hadn't done the night before.

The only other person in the room was Batalie. He looked up. "No recess, Tony?"

I said, "Some homework I didn't do last night."

"Always good to plan ahead."

For me, everything had extra meanings.

During lunch, it was a relief to sit with Lilly and her friends. Ian announced, as he had before, that his mother was making him a Penda Boy costume.

"So lame," said Philip. "This place is too full of Penda Boys."

"Don't care," insisted Ian. "My mother made a great velvet suit. Putrid green, like in the painting."

Madison asked Lilly about her costume.

She laughed and said, "It's a secret."

"Do you know?" Mia asked me, as if I should know.

"Nope."

"What are you going to be?" someone asked me.

"Haven't made up my mind."

For some reason they laughed. I suppose you've made friends when you say something normal and people laugh. There it was, I had finally made friends, but I couldn't tell them what was happening.

Back in class, it was about two o'clock when Batalie said, "Okay, class. Wednesday club time. You know where you're going."

The kids filed out. I hung back, but Jessica—manila envelope in hand—and Mac stood waiting for me at the door. I understood. They wanted to make sure I went to the meeting.

The Weird History Club was the only club that met in the cafeteria. No one was working in the kitchen. The air smelled of sour steam and soap. Empty food trays gleamed. A school janitor was swishing a mop over a wet floor, *slap*, *slap*.

"Okay," Jessica began, "we're going to review how we're going to get rid of the Penda Boy and save Tony. He's the only one who can see the Penda ghost. So Tony has to lead us to him in the towers."

"Which tower?" said Barney. He was nervously piling up sunflower-seed husks.

Jessica pulled out the building plans and laid them on the table. "Okay," she said, "here are the plans for the Penda School building when it was first built. I've been studying them."

"Cool," Mac said, as he chewed on a fingernail.

"See," said Jessica, pointing. "All these rooms—where servants lived—in the towers. Over here, passages and steps built into the walls."

"Awesome," said Barney, almost automatically.

They were all tense, twitchy, constantly sneaking glances at one another.

"Are they still there?" said Mac, as if reading the lines of a play.

Jessica pointed to a spot. "Here's a door right out of our homeroom."

"Perfect," said Barney.

"I'll pry it open," Jessica went on. "With people in costume wandering about, playing stupid games like ducking for apples, no one will know what we're doing. Soon as I get the door open"—she nodded at me—"you go through—seven o'clock—and since you've been studying the hidden passageways, you make your way."

I said, "Where am I supposed to go?"

Mac said, "Find the Penda Boy."

"Alone?" I said, though I had no doubt they would all be

waiting for me somewhere.

The others looked to Jessica.

"I'll be totally with you," she said.

Eyes shifted. I felt queasy.

"Cool," said Mac. He patted her arm.

"Well then," said Jessica, "that's the plan."

"But . . . ," I said, feeling I had to ask, "when—if—I find the Penda Boy, how . . . how do I deal with him before he . . . gets . . . me?"

"Good question," muttered Mac. No one spoke. We all turned to Jessica.

She said, "I googled 'How do you get rid of a ghost.'"

I couldn't believe she'd say something so stupid.

"It says you shine strong light on the ghost and point up. Or," she added, "burn sage leaves."

"What are sage leaves?" said Barney.

"Some kind of herb."

It was so idiotic I almost laughed.

Mac said, "The Halloween party goes from five thirty in the afternoon till eight."

"It'll be the best Weird History Club meeting ever," said Barney.

Jessica said, "I'll bring a chisel or a knife . . . for the door."

And for me, I thought.

Jessica said, "Does everyone have a way to tell the time?"

"Yeah."

"Great. Let's meet at the door at seven."

Mac said, "Wait! We have to know what costumes we're wearing, so we know how to find each other. I'm going to be a goblin."

"Troll monster," said Barney.

Jessica said, "Thought I'd be Mrs. Penda. You know, like that picture of her in the front office."

The hair at the back of my neck prickled.

Mac grinned and said, "I like that."

They all looked at me. Jessica said, "What are you going to be?"

"Not sure yet."

Jessica said, "Come on, Tony, you have to decide. We need to know what you'll look like. Otherwise things won't work."

"I'll get something," I said.

"Make it quick," Jessica snapped. "You've only got two days."

There was some uneasy talk about past Halloweens and what people wore. Happily, it wasn't long before the end-of-school bell rang.

"Good," said Jessica. "We're set. We're going to get rid of the Penda Boy."

She folded up the plans, put them in an envelope, and handed it to me. "Study them. You have to know the secret passages by heart. That way you'll know where to go."

When we got back to the classroom, though kids were there, Batalie was not. I assumed that too was planned, because Jessica went right to the back wall. She called Mac and me to come over.

"See?" she said, pointing.

I could see the faint outline of an old door.

She whispered, "It'll be easy to open."

"Any knife would do," said Mac.

Kids had already started to gather up their stuff and were leaving for the day. As Mac and Jessica drifted toward the door, I took my time.

From the doorway, Jessica called, "Tony, go work out your costume."

I said, "I will."

She gave me a thumbs-up and they left.

I waited a bit and then followed, determined to see where she went.

When I came out of school looking for Jessica, the morning's fog had thickened. The air was dank, the light ashen. Street colors were muted, the sharp edges of things blunted. The world out of focus. The combination of poor light and kids milling about on the sidewalk meant I couldn't spot Jessica at first. It was her height, black hair, and slight limp that allowed me to catch sight of her moving along the street. She was alone.

I ran across the street and, keeping back, followed. At the first corner, she made a right turn and then headed down the steep hill. I stayed behind, keeping to the left side of the street, behind the parked cars. She didn't seem to be in any great hurry, but she held a steady pace. It was easy enough to keep her in sight. Nor did she give the slightest sign to suggest she knew I was there.

The farther downhill we went, the thicker the fog. From the bay, foghorns began to moan. Hearing them, my dad had said, "The dead will soon rise."

How right he was.

When Jessica reached Lombard Street, six blocks down and at the base of the hill, I held back to see if she would get on a bus. A lumbering one arrived, then left, spewing black exhaust into the gloom. When it went on, Jessica crossed the street and kept walking, moving into the flat Marina District, toward the bay.

I walked faster, drawing as close as I dared. That slight

limp told me I was following the right person. A good thing too, because this was new territory to me, and the fog had intensified.

After six more long blocks, she reached what was called Marina Boulevard. She crossed it. Signs told me this was something called Marina Green. After some grass, there was a long waterside walkway with benches that faced the bay. Off to the left was a boat anchorage. The fog hung so low all I could see were lots of white hulls, which looked like the bellies of dead fish. Gulls, invisible in the overhead murk, squawked as if calling for help. Somewhere out in the bay was Alcatraz, but I couldn't see it.

I held back and saw Jessica—the only person there—sit down on one of the benches. Was this where she'd been going that time I saw her come out of the school? Why here?

As veils of gray mist whisked about her, she appeared to be doing nothing other than sitting and staring out at the water. Was she intending to *do* anything? I had no idea. But when a nearby foghorn suddenly bleated, she turned her head, as if curious to know where the sound came from. The roiling fog hid her briefly, then thinned, just enough for me to see her face.

The face I saw was not Jessica's face.

It was an old woman's face, long, narrow, and wrinkled,

with jutting chin, high cheekbones, and thin lips.

I was furious with myself. I had followed the wrong person. Frustrated, I turned away, only to hesitate. *Something* was familiar about the old woman.

Retreating some steps, I tried to see the woman through the fluid, fluctuating fog. Gradually, I realized who I had followed: the woman in the painting, Mrs. Penda. In other words, it was just as the Penda Boy had told me: Mrs. Penda and Jessica were one.

If she had turned in my direction, she would have seen me standing there, frozen with amazement. Fortunately, she shifted the other way.

Waking from my stupor, I backed off, going up the street only to stop, asking myself if what I had seen was really true. Perhaps this woman *was* someone else. Perhaps Jessica was wearing a mask she'd made for Halloween.

I turned around and crept back. She was still on the bench, her face sometimes visible, sometimes not. Motionless, hardly daring to breathe, I stood in place, watching, waiting—I didn't know for what.

It grew darker. Foghorns growled with increasing frequency, giving warnings. The mist turned to a cold drizzle. My fingers grew numb. Though I began to shiver, I remained where I was, staring. I had to be sure that what I was seeing was true.

The woman stood. I scurried across the boulevard, spying a bulky blue mailbox near the curb. I squatted behind it and peeked around, hoping she would not see me.

Mrs. Penda emerged out of the fog, limping the way Jessica did. As I watched, her old, wrinkled face began to twitch, shift, and alter, as if unseen hands were molding clay. All of a sudden I was looking at Jessica Richards, the young, pretty Jessica.

It was as if that youthful face was a mask, and she had come to take it off and let the cool, moist air soothe her real and ancient face, much the way I, with relief, took off my tie when I left school. She even—in that gesture I knew so well—pushed her black hair back behind an ear before going on. I had no doubt who she was.

She went past me, across Union Street, up Pacific Heights. I remained behind, darting from car to car, keeping her in view. Upon reaching the school, she opened the doors and disappeared inside. I remained on the sidewalk, gazing at the building, imagining her going into Ms. Foxton's office, stepping into the chest, descending those narrow steps into that awful room, lying on that decrepit bed.

I gazed up at the high tower. It was hidden in the fog the way everything in the Penda School was hidden.

❖ ❖ ❖

I tore home, shot into my apartment, locked the front door, double-locked it, went to my room, and sat at my desk, my head resting in my arms. It took a long time to calm down, to absorb what I had seen.

I was horrified.

I suppose it was thinking about her going to that room that gave me a new thought: When we had finished our Weird History Club meeting, Jessica had urged me to study the building plans, to learn them so I could know my way around. Since it was she and Bokor who had found a way to get the plans to me, I asked myself, were the plans accurate? Jessica assumed I had no knowledge of the private steps and rooms. Except I *had* learned something about them.

With the plans spread on my desk, it was easy to identify the front of the school, the reception hall. I was able to trace which old rooms had become the school office. That included Ms. Foxton's office.

I checked the spot where the chest stood.

No indication of steps leading down.

The room below, where I believed Jessica lived under Ms. Foxton's office, was not in the plans either.

Nor was there any suggestion of that meeting room, the

hallway, or the spiral steps that had led me up to the Penda Boy.

In other words, since the places I *did* know were *not* on the plans, I was sure the plans they had given me *had* been altered. No matter how much I studied them, once I walked through the door at the back of Batalie's room, I would be lost and at the mercy of Mrs. Penda and her friends. The best thing I could do was *not* study these plans.

Then I remembered: I still needed to tell the Penda Boy which door I would be going through. And the time. Otherwise, I would be going into those hidden passageways alone.

At dinner that night, Dad said, "Figure out your Halloween costume yet?"

"I'd like to be the Invisible Man."

Dad laughed. "That novel by H. G. Wells, *The Invisible Man*, was published the same year your school was founded."

I said, "I need a costume for the Halloween party. Can I have some money for that?"

Dad said, "Twenty bucks work?"

"Thanks."

Sitting at my desk, I reminded myself that I had promised to do two things—contrary things: I'd told the Penda Boy I would help him. I had told Jessica I would do what she and her Weird History Club wanted me to do.

My phone rang. Thinking it might be Jessica, I hesitated. When the ringing persisted, I couldn't resist.

"Hello . . ."

"Tony?"

To my relief, it was Lilly. "Hi."

"You'll never guess who called me."

"Who?"

"Jessica."

"What . . . what did she want?"

"She was being friendly. Said since she knew you and I were friends, and since she likes you a lot—said you were totally cool—that she and I should be friends too. That we, you know, should hang out together and do stuff at the Halloween party."

"Oh."

"I mean, I guess I wasn't being all that friendly to her, but I'm going to try to be nice. Just wanted you to know."

"Thanks."

"See you."

"Yeah."

I turned off the phone. I was sure Lilly hadn't understood, but the way I took it, it meant that if Jessica couldn't rip out my soul, she'd use Lilly. Did that mean Jessica suspected I knew more than I was saying? Or only that she had a backup plan?

I got on my slackline and tried to clear my head. When I kept falling, I got out that slackline book Uncle Charlie had given me and reread the first page of the book:

WARNING

Slackline can be dangerous, resulting in injury or possibly death.

I remembered Uncle Charlie saying: "When you walk the slackline, you're not in the air; you're not on the ground. Sort of half alive, half dead. Good practice for being a ghost."

I had to accept it: My becoming a ghost was what he'd been planning for me all along.

I had said, "I don't believe in ghosts."

He had laughed. "You will, someday."

"Someday?"

"When people say *someday*, it's like making a wish."

His wish.

I considered doing an Austin: quitting school. Only, if I did, they'd get Lilly. Lilly and me—not a romance, but she was my friend. If I skipped, they'd get her. The idea of Lilly being Jessica's servant horrified me. I didn't want that to happen, but the only way to prevent it was to have Jessica come after me.

I slept badly. I didn't mind the nightmares. At least when I woke up, they were gone. My problem was that the nightmares I faced when I awoke did not go away.

Thursday, the day before Halloween. I felt I was walking the line. The deadline. The line of the dead.

When I got up, my first thought was that I had to tell the Penda Boy about Jessica's plans. Only I couldn't face going to school. I had to think things out. So when I heard my folks move around the kitchen, I slumped to where they were, my pajamas still on.

Mom looked around. "What's the matter?"

"I feel sick."

She put her hand to my forehead. "You *are* a bit warm."

Dad said to me, "What do you think it is?"

"Don't know," I lied.

Dad, who never quite believed me when I claimed sickness, said, "Have any tests today?"

"Come on, Dad, I feel lousy."

My parents exchanged looks.

"I can't take time off today," said Mom.

"Neither can I," said Dad.

I felt like saying, *Nothing new there*. I didn't.

To me, Mom said, "You'll be alone."

"I'm used to it," I said.

Mom and Dad eyed each other. When Dad shrugged, Mom made the decision. "Okay, stay home. We don't want you getting worse."

"Thanks," I muttered, and went back to bed. Once there, I closed my eyes, not wanting to see the world.

Mom came to my room to say good-bye. "I called the school to tell them you weren't feeling well. That nice Mrs. Z said she hoped you'd get better so you won't miss the party tomorrow. I told her I was sure you'd be there. Call me if things get worse," she added, kissing my forehead.

Dad looked in. "Get well. You don't want to miss your Halloween party."

The front door shut. I heard the locks click.

I thought about Austin. Had he known as much as I did when he quit? Had he told his parents? Didn't matter. He got out. Once more, I considered doing the same. The Penda Boy had said Austin lacked courage. I thought he was smart. Yes, I wanted to save myself, but I felt I had to make sure

Lilly was not hurt. Besides, I kept telling myself, I wanted to get rid of Mrs. Penda.

If I told my parents, they would think I was insane.

If I told Lilly, she would think so too.

I remembered that old question, "What's the deal with Uncle Charlie?" The answer: he was trying to kill me. It made me shudder. I was glad I hadn't seen him for a while. Perhaps he had done his job—getting me to the school—and I'd never see him again. Good.

Somehow, I managed to sleep for a couple of hours.

It was near eleven when I woke. I was glad to be home, but I wished there were people in school I could talk to. I thought of Riley Fadden, the Student Council president. "Problems with the school," he had said, "come to me."

Not a chance.

I thought of Ms. Foxton. She had said, "If you can think of any way I can be helpful, my door is always open."

But . . . whose side was she on? The steps to Jessica's room were in her office. How could she *not* know?

I thought . . .

The first time we met, she'd looked at me with fear in her eyes, as if she was frightened of me. She'd even made a point of telling me not to believe stories about ghosts in the towers.

Warned me about Jessica. Made a big thing about finding me in the hall with her. Told Mom I should not hang around Jessica.

I tried to look at things differently: If Ms. Foxton *had* known what was going on when she first saw me, maybe she'd been fearful *for* me. She'd said Jessica didn't tell the truth. Made problems. She'd quoted someone who'd said, "A friend is one soul in two bodies." She had even added, "When choosing a friend, you might ask yourself: Do you wish to share souls with that person?" It was as if she *did* know about Mrs. Penda and what she did. That all along, she'd been trying to protect me from Jessica.

Then why hadn't she just told me?

Because—I answered myself—I saw her only in school. Because she could have no idea who might hear her tell me what was happening. Mrs. Z was sitting right outside her office, and both the Penda Boy and Jessica had told me she was a watchdog.

That brought on a new idea: maybe it was Ms. Foxton who'd found the dropped flashlight.

I figured out how it could have happened: That afternoon, she came back from her meeting and saw a backpack in the office. She asked Mrs. Z who it belonged to. Mrs. Z told her I'd been there.

No big deal.

But then Ms. Foxton goes into her own office and notices that the flashlight is gone. Thinks: someone has been in her office. Connects that with knowing *I* was in the *front* office. Wonders if I came into *her* office.

Discovers the letter opener on the floor by the chest. If she knows about Jessica, she knows about the chest.

She asks herself if *I* opened the chest. If I went below. She opens the lid. Easier to do from the top. She goes down the steps. Along the hallway. When she finds the flashlight at the bottom of the spiral steps, she knows what I have discovered— some of it anyway. That would explain why she called Mom, wanting to know if I got home. She was worried that I had been trapped down there. By telling Mom about my backpack, she knows I will go into the office and see the flashlight. In other words, the flashlight was a *message*. The message is: *I know what is going on.*

Then I remembered that time she had called Mom. When she did, she gave Mom her *private* number and told Mom that I should call her if I had things to talk about. Maybe that was another message missed.

I went over things repeatedly. It fit. At least I hoped so. But the only way I could be sure was by talking to her.

But if she *was* on my side, she couldn't talk to me at school.

Mrs. Z would hear. I had to find another way.

Mom had written that phone number on a yellow sticky note and given it to me. I rummaged around my messy desk but couldn't find it. I was sure I hadn't tossed it out, and my parents never touched my desk. I searched. It was nowhere.

I jumped on my slackline, walked back and forth, concentrating on what I was doing, not on the note. I got off and remembered. I had put the note in a book. *The Old Man and the Sea*.

I found the book. Found the private cell number. Should I call or not? I told myself I had to take the chance. I went into the living room, sat on the couch, and, using my cell phone, tapped out the number. It rang four times.

"This is Gloria."

"Is this . . . Ms. Foxton?"

"This is she." Her voice shifted. It became lower, stronger, professional. "Who is calling, please?"

"Tony Gilbert."

"Ah."

"I need to speak to you."

"Where are you?"

"Home sick. But not really."

"Ah," she said again.

"I'm alone."

There was some silence. Then she said, "What did you wish to talk to me about?"

"Your message." When she said nothing, I said, "The flashlight."

She stayed silent. I waited, my heart thumping. Then she said, "I'll see what I can do."

The phone went dead.

Did that mean she was coming or not? All I could do was wait. Wait to see if she would come. Wait to see if she was on my side.

An hour later, I heard a small tap on the front door. I jumped up and pulled it open. Ms. Foxton was standing there. She looked her usual self, a trim lady in a suit, her brown hair tied off at the back of her neck. Her face, however, had not even the hint of a smile.

The first thing she said was, "Where are your parents?"

"Working."

"Do they know you called me?"

"No."

"How much have you told them?"

"Nothing."

She remained unmoving, not crossing the threshold, as if

trying to decide what to do.

I said, "You know about Mrs. Penda, don't you?"

Her eyes swept over our apartment like she wanted to make sure no one else was there. She must have satisfied herself, because she gave a tiny nod—making a decision—and came forward.

"We can talk here," I said, gesturing toward our new couch. She sat down on the edge, feet together, hands clasped, eyes fixed on me. I sat across the way in an easy chair, not feeling easy.

Finally, she said, "Please tell me what you know."

I told her everything I had discovered about Jessica, the Penda Boy, the school, Bokor, Batalie, Mrs. Z, and what was going to happen during the Halloween party: that they were trying to get me to lead them to the Penda Boy because I was the only one who could see him. As soon as I got to him, they'd kill him—or whatever they do with someone half dead like him. Then they would take my soul. "It's what you said to me: 'A friend is one soul in two bodies.' That's what they want to do."

She grimaced.

I went on, telling her how if they couldn't get me, I was sure they would use someone. I didn't mention Lilly. I told her that they had to act by tomorrow night, their seven-year limit, their holy eve, Halloween, or they would be done.

As I talked, Ms. Foxton's eyes never left me. Now and again, she nodded as if to acknowledge what I said. A few times, such as when I told her about going into the tower and meeting with the Penda Boy, and how down by the bay I'd watched Jessica's face change, her eyes became wider. Mostly she listened.

When I was done she said, "I could cancel the party. Lock the school."

"The second they learn, they'd go after someone. Hate to tell you, but Jessica once told me, 'Someday I'm going to have to kill that woman.' She meant you."

The color faded from Ms. Foxton's face.

I said, "Did you know everything I told you?"

She nodded.

"For a long time?"

"I came to the Penda School two years ago."

"When did you find out?"

"Quite quickly. An unexpected meeting—as you might guess—with Mrs. Penda. I was told all I needed to know. Indeed, she insists I go to what she calls her board meetings. A normal school, except I learned that Mrs. Penda takes a student's soul every seven years. I suppose I didn't quite believe it until she went after Austin—I assume you know what happened to him."

I nodded.

"That's when I truly grasped it all. When I confronted Mrs. Penda—Jessica—she said that if I left the school, she would make sure I never worked again. She would have her board of trustees accuse me publicly of many things. When an adult works with young people, Tony, reputation is everything."

I thought of that long list of school heads. Now I knew why there were so many.

"Before I could decide what to do, you showed up at school to start classes. Until that morning, I hadn't even known you would be enrolled."

"Who told you?"

"Mrs. Penda. She told me you were about to become a student—replacing Austin. It was obvious to me that you had been picked as the next victim."

"But . . . who picked me?"

"Mrs. Penda said you'd been recommended by one of our former students—your great-uncle Charlie."

When I couldn't speak, she said, "I tried to warn you."

Recovering, I said, "You found the flashlight I dropped, right?"

"When I was at Mrs. Penda's meeting."

"You put it where I would see it so I would understand you knew."

"I hoped so. When I found it, I thought they might have already taken you."

"That's why you called my mother."

She nodded and then said, "Tell me what Mrs. Penda has planned."

"Tomorrow, at seven, I'm to go through the old door in the back of Mr. Batalie's room and lead her to the Penda Boy. She wants to destroy him."

"How will the boy protect you?"

"He wants me to go along with Jessica. When I go through the door, he'll hide me till midnight. If Jessica doesn't get what she wants, she'll go away, and so will the school."

"'Go away'?" Ms. Foxton asked faintly. "What does that mean?"

I shrugged. "Not sure."

"Can you trust him?"

"I don't have a choice."

"What do you wish me to do?"

All I could come up with was, "I guess . . . let me do what the Penda Boy wants."

"Aren't you frightened?"

I nodded.

"Are you going to tell your parents?"

"They won't believe me," I said. "If they did, they'd pull me out of school. Like Austin. If I go, the Weird History Club people will go after someone else. But it's me they want."

"Why?"

"There's something already dead in me."

Ms. Foxton was quiet for a while, and then she said, "You're very brave. Thank you."

We sat there, not speaking. Then she got up and went to the door. "If you can think of anything for me to do, please let me know." She left.

I walked the slackline for a long time. By the time I was done, I realized I had to see the Penda Boy before the party to tell him which door I was going through. And the time. I also wanted reassurance that he would be there.

The school librarian had told me she kept the library open for an hour after the end of classes. I'd go there and find the Penda Boy, somehow. If anyone asked what I was doing, I'd say I felt better and needed to work on Bokor's term paper. It was due tomorrow.

I was about to leave when my phone rang.

"Lilly?"

"You okay?"

"Not feeling great."

"Not going to miss the Halloween party, are you?"

"I'll be there."

"Pick your costume yet?"

"Still thinking. You?"

She laughed. "As I told you, it's a secret."

I had left the apartment and was on the street going toward school when my phone rang again.

"Hello."

"What's happening?" It was Jessica, her voice tight.

"Nothing, really. Stomachache. I'm good."

"Great. So you'll be at school tomorrow, right? For the party?" I could hear her relief.

"Sure."

"Figure out your costume?"

"Still thinking."

"Tony, you have to let us know in the morning."

"I will."

I was almost at school when the phone rang a third time.

"Hello?"

"Hi. It's Mom. How are you feeling?"

"Lot better."

"Oh good. Wouldn't want you to miss your big Halloween party."

"Nope."

"What are you doing now?"

"Taking it slow."

"Great. See you soon. Love you."

"Love you."

I suspect her reaction would have been different if I had told her I was going to meet a ghost.

Once I got to the school, I stopped and studied the building. It was so strange: old, oddly shaped, with turrets, towers, and multiple roofs. It made me think how when you look at a building—any building—you never know what's going on inside. The outside of a building is a mask. A Halloween mask.

I looked up toward the window in the tall tower. Within seconds, the Penda Boy was there. We stared at each other. Then he vanished. I hoped he sensed my need to speak to him.

I had thought the school would be deserted. Nothing like. There were many people—parents for the most part, moms, with a few kids—busily putting up Halloween decorations for the big party. Strangest was the reception hall, where they were laying out a fake cemetery, complete with gravestones for every teacher. I saw Ms. Foxton's name, Batalie's, others.

There was even one with the name Mrs. Penda on it.

They had no idea the school was already a cemetery. Just no one was underground.

Unlike the rest of school, the library was deserted. Not even the librarian was there. No decorations either. Just afternoon sunlight piercing the old chapel windows, causing dust motes to swirl gently in bars of rainbow air. On the tables, abandoned books. *Nothing is quieter, or has more secrets*, I thought, *than a book that's closed.*

Deciding I had to make a show of working—in case someone came in—I sat at a table, grabbed a book, and opened it. Not that I read anything. I was waiting for the Penda Boy.

As I sat there, the room shook. A book popped out of one of the cases and landed on the floor with a thump. Another earthquake. They *were* getting stronger. I struggled to read the book in my hands. After a few pages, I looked up. Sitting at the other side of the table was the Penda Boy.

He said, "You wanted to see me."

"Tomorrow, at seven o'clock, Jessica wants me to go through the door at the back of Mr. Batalie's room."

"Do it. When you come through, I'll be on the other side so I can hide you. Of course, they'll try to find you. I'll keep them looking for you until midnight. Once we get past that, they can no longer exist."

"And . . . you'll really be there?" I asked.

Instead of answering, he vanished.

He must have heard Mrs. DuBois, the librarian, because she walked in. "Why, hello, Tony," she said. "I didn't expect anyone this afternoon. Such excitement. Did you find what you needed?"

"Yes, thank you." I stood up.

"This will be your first Penda Halloween. What are you going to be?"

"Not certain," I said, and meant it.

Leaving school, I made my way through the reception-hall cemetery and then headed downhill. In a big Walgreens on Union Street, I went to the Halloween section. Tons of people were there, adults and kids. There was the usual display of masks: Frankenstein, witches, monsters, and bizarre animals. It took some searching before I found a mask I liked, one with no facial features. Even the eyeholes were white gauze. A blank mask. It cost the twenty bucks Dad had given me.

A mirror allowed me to look at myself. I was a ghost. Was that what I'd look like after tomorrow?

The next day, Friday, Halloween, was supposed to be a regular school day. It was not. Kids were very excited. They loved the reception-floor cemetery. There seemed to be a tradition of putting flowers on your favorite teacher's grave. Guess which one had the most flowers? Mrs. Penda's.

During classes, nobody paid attention. Even the teachers were keyed up. In history, Bokor collected the papers that were due in a box that was passed around. I put in nothing. I figured either he or I would not be around to deal with it.

As we left class, he cried, "Halloween, my friends. Keep hold of your souls."

People laughed.

I didn't.

During recess, I felt I had to sit with the Weird History Club: Jessica, Mac, and Barney. I hoped I'd show nothing of what I felt or knew.

The boys were tense, restless. Jessica's eyes showed excitement. "Are we set?" she asked, like a coach telling a team to go out there and win.

"I am," said Barney. "You, Tony?"

"I'm good."

"What's your costume?" Jessica asked.

"A ghost," I said.

Their eyes shifted to one another, as if not sure how to respond.

"What kind of ghost?" Jessica demanded.

I shrugged. "An ordinary one."

No one spoke until Jessica said, "Just make sure we're the only ones who know who you are." She stood up. "Okay, guys. Seven o'clock. Batalie's room."

Barney said, "Cool."

During lunch, I sat with Lilly and her friends. No matter what anyone said, there were gales of laughter.

Lilly turned to me. "Do you have your costume?"

It was the same question that Jessica had asked. I said, "Yeah."

"What?"

"If you're not telling, I'm not."

Not exactly funny, but everybody laughed.

When school ended at three, everyone left to hide inside their costumes.

The party would start at five thirty.

Once home, I tried to walk my slackline but kept falling.

At about a quarter to five, my folks got in. "We wanted to see your costume," Dad announced.

"Can I borrow one of your white shirts?" I asked. Mom found an old one of Dad's, which she gave to me, asking, "What are you going to be?"

"I'll show you."

Dad's shirtsleeves covered my hands, which I liked. I put on some baggy white pants, then a pair of whitish sneakers, and finally my blank mask.

I studied myself in the mirror. Except for my scruffy brown hair, with no mouth and no eyes I was a blank.

I walked in on my folks.

"A ghost!" cried Dad. "Love it."

"Looks like fun," said Mom. "When do you have to be there?"

"It starts soon."

"When will you be back?"

"It's supposed to end at eight," I said, careful not to say when I would return. Actually, I didn't know when—or if—I'd be back.

"Should I pick you up?" asked Mom.

"I'll call," I said.

"Have fun, Mr. Ghost," said Mom.

Dad called, "Come back alive."

I muttered, "Someday," and left our apartment.

It was almost five thirty when I set out for school, mask in hand. Daylight was dwindling. In the east, a half-moon hung low. To the west, a few crimson clouds cut across the sky like bleeding wounds. Streets were crowded with Friday night traffic, horns beeping like a cell phone test center.

I saw lots of little kids dressed up: Spider-Man, a cowboy, Darth Vader, a witch, one little kid in a full-size 49ers helmet. He looked like a mushroom with legs. Most of these kids were with parents.

About a block from school, I began to see bigger kids in costumes so elaborate I couldn't tell who they were. I halted, put on my mask, and went on.

As I reached the school steps, cars were pulling in. More costumed kids were climbing out. It was clear they had spent a lot of time and money.

I headed into school and found myself saying—under my breath—Uncle Charlie's last words: "Here we go."

When I stepped inside the school, an adult dressed in a tuxedo with a face painted bloodred pinned a number on me. "For the costume contest," it was explained.

The scene at school was incredible. Call it a fantasy animation movie gone wild, or your worst nightmare. First there was the fake cemetery. Then it was like a costume store come to life. Name any movie or TV character. Think of the animals on Noah's ark. Think of every movie monster, from Godzilla to your favorite space alien. They were there. Even famous people had come, like an Abraham Lincoln with a green face and fangs plus George Washington with a bloody hatchet buried in his head, dripping scarlet gore.

As creatures ambled about the reception-hall cemetery, strobe lights flickered and the sound system blared sounds of fake thunder, lightning, and rain, followed by wicked laughter, screeches, owl hoots, and eerie music. The great chandelier had even been hung with tiny red beads—meant, I supposed, to be drops of blood.

Everything was fake death, of course, but I knew that some of the fake was real. Amid the zany zombies and glittery ghosts, six really dead souls were mingling, intent on staying alive for the next seven years by feasting on me. And there I was, a pretend ghost, about to deal with real ghosts bent on real death. A circus of the weird. I had to ask myself: Which *weird* was going to be for me, "strange" or "fate"?

My costume was one of the simplest, and probably the cheapest. Still, I doubted if anyone knew who I was any more than I could tell who was who behind their disguises. I could guess which ones were teachers, because they were bigger than most of the kids. Not that I could put names to them. I assumed Ms. Foxton was there, but wasn't sure. Nor could I figure out if Batalie, a small adult, was there.

I had no idea who Lilly was. Same for her best friend, Mia. She had told us she was going to be a clown, but in all the horror, there was a crowd of gory clowns.

I caught sight of a Penda Boy, then four more in as many minutes. All wore green suits, lace collars, high-button shoes, and blond wigs, so like the painting. Who the kids were, I had no idea because faces were painted green, red, or blue. Then, as I wandered around, I saw Mrs. Penda.

She was standing halfway up one of the main staircases as if surveying the scene. She looked exactly like her painting, except that the number seven was pinned to her sleeve. Considering where she stood, it occurred to me that either she wanted to be noticed, or she was looking for me. Not that anyone paid special attention to her. She appeared as one odd character among all the others. But having seen her down by the bay a few days before, I was sure she was the real Mrs. Penda, which is to say Jessica.

It struck me: she had the best disguise of all. She was the only one who came as herself. And nobody knew it.

Except me.

Or so I thought. Because then I saw a *second* Mrs. Penda, this one with the number seventy-seven on her sleeve. She too looked so like the Mrs. Penda in the painting, I no longer knew who the real one was, or if either one was. All I knew was that Mrs. Penda *was* there, waiting to grab me.

Though restless, wanting to get things going, I roamed about. Like everyone else, I approached this costumed person, then another, peering at them, trying to guess who was who. At the same time, people kept coming up to me and asking, "Who are you?" I turned away—as they did—not answering.

I did see a troll and, because of his size, decided it was Mac. Not that I was sure. There were a number of short ugly goblin creatures too, one of which had to be Barney. Enormous Mr. Bokor was not hard to find. He was costumed all in black, including a black cape and a black top hat. He had painted his face blue, with yellow streaks running from his eyes.

For a while people milled around, showing off. I supposed we were being judged for best costume. At some point, I realized that the Mrs. Pendas were gone. So was Bokor. I had not found Lilly. That worried me.

A voice rang out over the speaker system. "Let the games begin."

I actually shuddered.

The speaker voice went on. "Apple ducking in the first-grade room. Flip ball in the fourth-grade room." Other games were mentioned. If I heard it right, there were no games in Batalie's room. Jessica had arranged everything.

People began to move out of the reception-hall area. Some went down the hall, while others headed for the second floor. I made my way up too. Once there, I walked to the far end of the hall, Batalie's room. Number seven.

I stood in front of the shut classroom door and looked back along the hall. At the other end, I saw costumed kids wandering in and out of various rooms. No one was near me.

Certain I wouldn't be noticed, I opened the door. It was dark inside. I felt around the door frame until my fingers felt a switch. I flicked it up. Lights came on. It was deserted. My eyes went right to the door at the back. It was ajar.

Jessica had done what she had promised to do.

I hoped the Penda Boy would.

I shut the classroom door behind me, stepped forward, and surveyed the room. It all looked ordinary. Papers on Batalie's desk were arranged neatly, topped by his reading glasses. On the comment board, student portraits were lined up. It took a moment for me to realize that my picture had been removed. The realization gave me goose bumps.

I went to that door on the back wall. It was narrower than modern doors, and not as tall. Chips of white paint were scattered on the floor like confetti—but not for a party. A few feet from the door, on the floor, lay a knife. I assumed Jessica had used it to get the door open. Since it was also probably what she was going to use on me, I picked it up and gingerly felt the edge. It was very sharp.

Hurriedly setting the knife down on a chair, I used both hands to pull the door open wide on its stiff hinges in hopes the Penda Boy would be there. He was not. But I was struck by how different the two sides of the door were. The class side was smooth and white. The far side had an old-fashioned glass doorknob and a latch meant to keep the door closed. It was also filthy, matted with shaggy strands of dirt-encrusted cobwebs in which lay mummified flies. Life on one side of the door, death on the other.

Light from the classroom allowed me to see some of what lay beyond that door: a short hallway, not so very different from what I had seen that time I was in Jessica's basement room. Warped wooden floor and walls. A low ceiling made of the same material. The hallway didn't go far but veered to the left. The air was dusty.

I was not sure what to do. The Penda Boy had told me that once I went through the door, he'd be waiting for me. He wasn't. For that matter, Jessica had also said she'd be with me when I went through. She hadn't arrived either.

I had one last moment to escape. I didn't. I had to go through with it.

Leaving the door ajar, I took out my phone and checked the time. It was about ten minutes before seven. In an odd way it was reassuring that I was early.

I grabbed a chair and set it near the door so I could keep watch. Once I was there, it took all my strength and resolve to sit down and try to be calm. My sole hope was that the Penda Boy would appear before Jessica.

Wanting to keep watch on the time, I put my phone on the chair next to the knife. Hot, tense with waiting, I took off my mask and rolled up my long sleeves. My eyes kept shifting from that little hallway to the time on my phone. And the knife.

The room shook, hard. Books sprang from shelves. A few desks slid along the floor. The earthquakes were becoming ever more powerful.

I heard what sounded like an announcement blaring from the school's speaker system. I assumed it was some game thing. Or perhaps the contest for the best costume had been decided. Not caring, I stayed where I was, concentrating on the time. I toyed with the knife. I put it down. I fidgeted. The minutes on my phone changed very slowly. As it happened, I had been sitting there for a while, trying hard not to think, when I heard a sound behind me.

I spun about. It was a clown. It took a moment for me to realize it was Mia, Lilly's best friend.

"Hi," I said.

"Tony!" she cried breathlessly. "Oh my God, have you seen Lilly?"

"Don't know what costume she's wearing. Why?"

"Didn't you hear?"

"Hear what?"

Mia was panting. "Something's happened to Ms. Foxton. She's had an accident. Or worse. Nobody knows what happened. Oh my God, it's awful."

I stared.

"Didn't you hear the announcement?" Tears trickled down, smearing her smiling clown face, making her look grotesque. "The party is canceled," she said. "We're supposed to go right home, but I was going to stay with Lilly. Only I can't find her. She said she wanted to find out who was dressed as Mrs.

Penda. But she never came back. Why are you sitting in here? Is that back door open?"

I said, "Did you say she went to find Mrs. Penda?"

"Tony, I have to find Lilly." She moved toward the outer door. "You better go. If you find Lilly, *please* tell her to call my phone, okay? Please."

"What was Lilly's cos—"

She ran out.

Following her out of the room, I watched her run down the deserted hallway. From afar, I heard shouts, and screams.

What happened to Lilly?

The sound system blared, "All students must leave the building immediately. No exceptions. Remain calm, but move quickly. The Halloween party is canceled. All students must leave the building immediately. Please leave." Lights began to blink out. Darkness was advancing along the hallway—toward me.

At that moment—more than at any other time—I considered running out of the school. Instead, I forced myself to go back into the classroom, to the back door. I peered into the small hallway. No Penda Boy. I checked my phone. When I saw that it was 6:59, I shifted around to face the classroom door, just in time to see Mrs. Penda—the number seven still pinned to her sleeve—walk into the room.

She was not alone. Behind her was Bokor. So were Mrs. Z and Batalie. So were Barney and Mac. And, standing next to Mrs. Penda, was Uncle Charlie.

Smiling, Uncle Charlie looked just the way he had that Sunday morning when I first saw the school—and all times since: an old pot-bellied guy, gray hair flopping over his forehead, dressed in a checkered shirt, tan suspenders, jeans, and loafers, the tassels still in place.

"Hello, Tony," he said in that croaky voice I knew so well. "I'm *so* glad I can talk to you again. I must apologize. I didn't want to *tell* you what to do. Not a good thing to do with kids your age. Just wanted to keep you moving forward."

It was his seeming so regular, so normal, that shocked me. I had to tell myself that he was dead, a ghost, and was trying to become alive by taking my soul.

Unable to say anything, I simply stared at him.

He made a casual gesture. "This is my friend Mrs. Penda. A long time ago, she and I went to school together. I want you to know it was I who suggested to Mrs. Penda that you become a student here. I told Mrs. Penda you would be perfect. And I was right. Oh, Tony, I just wanted to come back to life and have more fun. We did have fun, didn't we?

"Do you remember," he went on, "my words just before I

died? What Albert Einstein said? 'The distinction between past, present, and future is only an illusion.' So here we are. You might say Mrs. Penda is past. I'm the present. And you're the future. I do hope you're feeling pleased."

What I felt was an overwhelming feeling of betrayal and rage.

While he spoke, Mrs. Penda looked on, her face severe, lips clenched tightly, cheekbones hollow, black hair piled atop her head, the air reeking of her sweet, musty perfume. Only when Uncle Charlie stopped speaking did she cover her face with both hands. They were an old woman's hands, thin-fingered, wrinkled, with swollen knuckles and cracked, yellowing nails.

But when she took her hands away, those wrinkles began to melt, the knuckles to smooth, the fingers became youthful. She became the young Jessica again, the pretty Jessica. She loosened her hair and let it fall about her face, pushed a strand behind her ear, while offering up one of her most dazzling smiles. She was evil one moment, my best friend the next. It was all so impossible.

"Now, Tony," she said, "aren't you glad your uncle Charlie brought you here? Did we amaze you?"

When I still didn't answer—I couldn't—she said, "I guess I did surprise you. I hate to tell you, your ghost costume is so fake. And I know how much you hate fake. I thought you would have understood by now: ghosts are real. And we're going to give you the opportunity to be a real one."

By her side stood Mac, costumed as a troll, and Barney, in a stupid goblin outfit, holding some kind of knurly club. Looming behind was Bokor. The blue and yellow on his face had fused, giving him a dark green hue, as if he were rotting. Perhaps he was.

Batalie was there too, costumed like some idiot pirate. Mrs. Z stood by his side, small in her trim black suit, her face childishly painted with cat whiskers. A revolting couple.

"Did . . . did my parents know what you were doing?" I managed to say to Uncle Charlie.

"Of course not!" he cried, his eyes positively merry. "We never did bother about them, did we? You and me, Tony, we're the real family, remember?"

I said, "You lied to me."

"Now, Tony," he said, "I asked you if it wouldn't be great if we went to the other side, together. And you said, 'Sure.' So I arranged it. Don't you think that's great? While I'm not fond of Ms. Foxton, I was in the room when she quoted that Greek philosopher, Aristotle, to you. I *loved* what she said: 'A friend is one soul in two bodies.' That's exactly the way you and I were, Tony. Right from the moment I moved in with you and your parents, I wanted us to be together, *forever.* You and me, one soul, two bodies. Well, eight bodies, actually. Doesn't that make you happy?"

"What happened to Lilly?" I asked. "And Ms. Foxton?"

Mrs. Penda said, "Ms. Foxton has been fired."

"Did you kill her?"

"Schools are complicated," said Bokor. "They require an enormous amount of cooperation. If the head of school doesn't work well with the teaching staff—doesn't have their full trust—you might say the school dies. We need the school to continue."

Then Mrs. Z said, "And Tony, we know Ms. Foxton went to your home. Visiting students without parents being present is completely against school regulations. My goodness. It's against state law."

"Are you the law?" I said.

"This is my school!" Jessica cried. "It's for me. Without me it's nothing. It would vanish."

"What about Lilly?"

Jessica laughed. "Your friend is not very smart. She wanted to know who I was. I showed her. She's safe as long as you cooperate. She's our backup."

From where I was standing, against the wall, I was able to dart a look into the hallway behind the door, which was open a few inches. I was desperately hoping the Penda Boy would be there. He was not.

"Now then," Jessica went on, "first things first: You must lead us to the Penda Boy. He has this nasty trick of allowing only one person to see him. We have to deal with him first. He interferes far too much. Then we'll take your soul and share it among ourselves, your uncle Charlie included. Which is only fair, don't you think?

"When we're done, you and your uncle Charlie will be one of us, students at Penda for as long as you like. We'll have so much fun being in first grade again. And we'll have honored the past and protected the future."

She distracted me with one of her splendid smiles, so that before I realized what she was doing, she took a quick step forward and snatched up the knife from the chair. "Ready? Now go through the door and find that stupid boy."

I stood there.

Uncle Charlie took a step toward me, his hand extended. "Come on, Tony, you and I were always a team. This is your reward."

I stole another look into the hallway. That time, at the far end, I caught sight of the Penda Boy. Moreover, I knew I was the only one who could see him.

"Good boy," said Uncle Charlie, taking another step toward me.

That was when I bolted through the doorway.

Once on the far side, I reached back and slammed the door shut. Fumbling, I hooked the latch—knowing it wouldn't hold them longer than a moment—then ran down the hallway toward the Penda Boy. The only light came from his glow. It wasn't much, but it allowed me to go toward him.

"This way!" he cried, and turned and raced around the bend. He made no sound, though my running made an awful clatter.

From behind I heard a crash, and I assumed the door I'd come through had given way. "They're through the door!" I shouted.

The Penda Boy didn't pause, but kept on until we came into a small, dim room. Empty and dilapidated, it had three doors. He went to one, pulled it open, called, "Hurry," and went through. Yanking the door shut behind me, I tried to stay close. I took two steps, tripped, and went sprawling.

"Get up! Get up!" the boy screamed.

Although my knees stung and my left ankle hurt, I forced myself up. Limping, I ran after him. From behind I heard doors slam and the sound of feet running in many directions.

We reached some steps. The Penda Boy clambered up. I followed as best I could until we came to a landing with two doors. He chose one and went through. I stayed with him.

A little way on, I stopped. My ankle was hurting. I was out of breath. Footfalls sounded above and below. I had the sense that we were being surrounded. "Where are we?" I called.

"We mustn't stay here!" he cried, and hurried on. I forced myself up and struggled to keep him in view. When he reached a hole in the floor, he appeared to jump into it, and disappeared. I drew up to the same place and peered down, relieved to see him scurrying down a steep staircase.

I hooked my legs over, grabbed what I thought was a railing, and started after. It was so dark I had to feel my way. He was waiting at the last step—not that I knew where that was. Nor did he say anything, though his glow pulsed rapidly, as if agitated.

"I have to rest," I said, sitting on the last step. My breath was coming in gasps, my chest hurt, and my ankle was full of shooting pains.

"You can't stop until we're a little farther," he said. When he darted away, I limped after him.

He came to a flight of steps going up. Instead of using them— as I expected—he went behind the steps, into a triangular alcove backed by a small wall. Squeezing his child's fingers around that wall's edge, he pried the wall open. Behind was a tiny space, no more than four feet deep and wide, with a steeply slanted ceiling.

"They don't know about this," he whispered. "We can hide here and wait. I've done it before."

Pressing my back, he urged me into the space. When I entered the space, he followed, pulling the wall piece closed after us. I managed to sit, but only by pulling up my knees and leaning my head forward, a painfully cramped position. He sat beside me. As he did, his light faded until the alcove became as dark as night.

After a while I said, "Do you know what's happened?"

"No."

"They've done something to Ms. Foxton. I don't know what. And . . . and that old man you saw, he's my uncle Charlie. He was the one who arranged for me to come to the school. He . . . wants my soul too." Only then did the full dreadfulness of it grip me. Tears slid down my face. I tried to stop them, but they kept coming. I had to gulp for air.

All the Penda Boy said was, "If we can stay free till midnight, they'll all disappear."

"They have Lilly."

"Lilly?"

"I told you. She's a friend. A girl in my class. If they can't take me, they'll use her."

"That makes things harder for them, and us." He was silent for a moment. Then he said, "Where is she?"

"No idea." When we continued to sit there, I said, "What are we going to do?"

As if trying to decide, he remained quiet. After a while he said, "We need to free her. If they use her—and they could— we'll never be rid of them. It's you we want them searching for. We still have time."

I asked, "Do you have any idea where they would put her?" It was easier to think of protecting her than myself.

He said, "There are too many rooms."

"In the tall tower?" I pressed, that being one of the few places I knew.

"If you go there and they come after you, you'll be trapped."

"What about their meeting room?" I offered. "Near Jessica's room?"

He seemed to consider that for a moment. "It's worth a try," he said. "But we need to take our time."

"Why?"

"We should wait until it's closer to midnight."

"But that's five hours, and Lilly is—"

"Shh."

I heard running footsteps. Neither of us spoke. I held my breath. They passed by.

He whispered, "Best not to speak anymore."

I reached for my phone, only to realize I'd left it in Batalie's room.

The Penda Boy was silent.

I don't know how long we stayed there. All the while, the Penda Boy remained motionless and quiet. I fidgeted. When I did, he'd hiss, "Don't."

Now and again, as from a great distance—above, below—I heard knocking, banging, footfalls. Sometimes the space we were in shook. My thoughts wandered. At some point I said, "May I ask something?"

"If you must."

"Why did Mrs. Penda make this school?"

"Growing older, she became appalled by the prospect of death. Trying to find ways of becoming young again, she met Bokor, who taught her how to stay young. It's as I told you. They steal the soul of a young person and she becomes six again. Never graduates, but starts school anew. Then, when she becomes twelve—seventh grade—she must take another soul.

"If you are to stay young forever, what better place to hide than in a school? If you are going to steal a young person's soul, what better place to find one than in a school?"

"And you were the—"

"Shh," he said. More footsteps came and went. "No more talk," he insisted. "Sleep to pass the time."

"You won't leave me . . ."

"No."

Thinking that if I slept the boy might abandon me, I remained unmoving in that tight, silent darkness. Full of worry, limbs numb from being so cramped, I struggled to stay awake. Even so, I slid into shallow sleep.

"Wake up."

From the darkness of my sleep, I woke to the darkness of our hiding place.

"What is it?"

"We have to move."

"Why?"

"It's getting close to midnight."

"How do you know?"

"If I know anything, it's time. They are becoming desperate. If we are to save your friend . . ."

"Tell me what to do."

He started to glow again, which allowed me to see him

again. "Just keep close to me."

Moving cautiously, he pushed open the wall he had used to enclose us and crawled out. I came after. We stood up, my legs tingling from being so cramped. He moved his head this way and that, like a bird listening.

Quite suddenly, he began to scamper down a narrow hallway. Desperate not to lose sight of him, I kept up as best I could.

He went around one corner, and then another. It was like finding our way through a maze. I tried to be quiet, but, stiff from all my sitting, I lumbered.

He stopped and waited until I had caught up. "We need to go there," he said, and pointed to a hole in the floor. It was a spiral stairway. For all I knew, it was the one I had climbed before. He started down. Gripping the rail to keep from falling, I followed.

I don't know how far we went. It seemed endless. When we finally reached the end, I had no sense of where we were. All I could see was another hallway.

"My ankle really hurts," I whispered, sitting on the last step. I listened hard. Beyond my thudding heart, my gasping breath, I heard creaking and groaning, as if the walls about me were shifting, altering. In addition, though it came as if from a great distance, I was quite sure I heard my name called. "Tony! Tony!"

It sounded like Uncle Charlie's voice. I looked to the Penda Boy. He too appeared to be listening. All he said was, "Are you ready?"

"For what?"

"To save your friend."

"Where are we?" I asked.

"Not far from Mrs. Penda's room."

"Under Ms. Foxton's office?"

He nodded. "Your suggestion. Near that meeting room."

I started to move. He held up a hand. "Someone's close." He made a motion with his head, which I understood to mean *down the hallway*.

"Is it Lilly?"

"Hopefully." He looked at me. "You have to deal with it."

"Me?"

"She won't be able to see me. If I changed that, I don't how she would react. Better for me to stay behind as much as possible—for now."

I sat there.

"If you wish to save her, you must hurry," he pressed.

I stood and stared down the hallway. It was dark save for some indistinct fluttering light some way along. I was not sure what it was or where it came from. As far as I could see, the hallway was deserted.

"Go," he pressed.

I went forward a few steps, paused, and looked back. The Penda Boy—his body glowing faintly—was standing where I had left him, watching me. He waved me forward. I went on. The more I moved down the hall, the harder it was to see him, and the more I felt alone.

A sudden jolt—as if a sledgehammer had struck—made the whole area shudder. Debris rained from the ceiling. The hall, already murky, became even more obscured as filth clogged the air. It was so thick I had to cover my nose and mouth with a hand. As it was, I was coated with plaster dust. *Earthquake*, I decided, aware that this one had had even more strength than previous ones.

The air around me, saturated with so much junk, was hard to see through. I wiped my face and cleared my eyes. I had to put a hand to a wall to guide myself. The other hand I kept over my nose and mouth.

I glanced back again and saw the Penda Boy, or just his form. He had become coated with dust. But, feeling great urgency, I continued on.

As I advanced, I realized that the fluttering light I'd noticed was seeping into the hallway from the left. I tried to think why it wasn't steady. Then I remembered that on the meeting room table there had been a candle. If it was lit, that might explain the light's irregularity.

I crept forward, reached out, and felt a corner. With as much caution as I could muster, I peeked around. I had guessed right. It was the small alcove near Jessica's room, the one that led to that meeting room. The door was closed, but that trembling light leaked around it, making it appear as if the door was framed with fire.

I looked back down along the hallway. The Penda Boy was no more than a shadow. Even so, I was certain he was still waving me on. The whole area lurched. More fragments cascaded down.

I waited until the air settled before stepping into the alcove. As I did, I heard from behind me an eruption of loud noises: thumps and thuds, followed by an unspeakable scream of pain. Then came an unearthly shriek, long and high-pitched, full of the most dreadful agony. Afterward came absolute silence, as awful as anything I had just heard.

Knowing only that something ghastly had occurred—but having no idea what—I came out of the alcove and looked back along the hallway from which I had come. Wanting reassurance, I hoped to see the Penda Boy. All I saw were shifting shadows, like fluttering black flames.

I don't know how long I stood there, staring, trying to grasp what had happened—I kept hoping it was only the thick air that obscured my view, that the Penda Boy was all right, that he hadn't abandoned me or been attacked. I could not tell.

I waited for the air to settle. It did, some, but I was still unable to see the boy. Undecided if I should go back, if he needed me, if I could help, I strained to hear. There was nothing but silence.

Telling myself I must go forward—believing the boy could take care of himself—I went into the alcove. Using both hands, I grabbed the door handle and gave it a jerk. The door popped open.

On the table, as I had guessed, was a burning candle; the flame's light was streaming like a painted star in the dust-laden air. Standing by the table was a short, ugly green creature. Instantly, I was sure it was Barney. Even as I decided it was him, I saw, sitting in a corner chair, hands behind her back, a cloth tied over her mouth, Mrs. Penda.

Bewildered, I just stood there, staring at her. That's when Barney lurched toward me, club in hand, held up as if to strike. It was enough to bring me back to life. I sprang forward, pinned his arms, and ripped the stick away. With a horrible snarl, he broke free and came at me again.

Wanting only to defend myself, I lashed out at him with the stick. Between his forward movement and my swing, the stick struck his face with great force, shattering it like a pot of clay.

Bits of his face fell to the floor. It was as if I had smashed his mask apart. Underneath, a different face was revealed. It wasn't Barney's face or, for that matter, anyone, or any*thing*, I knew. It was the face of an old, decaying man, shriveled and wrinkled, with red, runny eyes and a collapsed, toothless mouth. A few strands of moist, lank hair hung from his bald, blue-veined head, from which blood and pus oozed.

Though shocked by what I saw, I held the club aloft, ready to hit out again. In that instant, Barney dashed past me and fled from the room. I heard a bell ringing—I assumed it was Barney sounding an alarm. That was followed by the sound of many bells from many places, some close, some far.

I turned back to Mrs. Penda. Holding up the candle, I drew closer. Only then did I realize that she was Lilly, in costume.

I yanked the cloth from her mouth.

She coughed and managed to gasp, "Tony, oh my God." Then, confused: "Please, help me. I want to go home."

"Don't talk," I said, not wanting anyone to hear us.

I twisted around the chair she was sitting on and worked frantically to pry apart the knots by which she was bound.

When I had them loosened, she grabbed me with two hands and stood up, or at least tried.

"We've got to hurry!" I cried.

Leading her by one hand, the lit candle in my other, I guided us out of the room. Once in the hallway—the sound of bells ringing all around us—I turned to the left, which I knew would lead us to Jessica's room. That was the only way out I knew—*if* we could get up the steps and out of the chest.

When I reached the door, I kicked at it as hard as I could, not knowing who or what would be on the other side. The door fell in. Candlelight showed me no one was there.

"Come on," I called, and went to the foot of those old, narrow steps.

No sooner did we reach them than the whole room gave another violent shake. With a crash, the freestanding closet toppled over, breaking into pieces.

"What's happening?" gasped Lilly.

I said what I had begun to think: "The school is collapsing."

I held up the candle. The steps were still intact. Even better, the chest door above appeared to be open, which meant we could get into Ms. Foxton's office.

"This way." I hurried up. Lilly came after me. Near the

top, I peered out of the false chest into the office. Two of the chairs were overturned, and Ms. Foxton's desk was covered with hunks of plaster. The fireplace had buckled. The photograph behind the desk of joyful kids had fallen. A few cabinet doors had slid open. File folders had spewed onto the floor. But no one was there.

I helped Lilly out of the chest. "This way," I said, and guided her to the outer office. The painting of Mrs. Penda had fallen off the wall, its frame broken, the canvas curled and twisted on the couch. The Penda Boy painting was still up, but was hanging crookedly.

I pushed the office door open. As I did, the room quaked. The painting of the Penda Boy crashed to the floor, facedown.

We stepped into the reception hall. No one was there. The fake cemetery was a shambles. The chandelier was swinging wildly. Though mostly still lit, little lights were falling like the final bits of a Fourth of July rocket. The area was darkening rapidly.

Just able to see the front doors, I shouted, "Come on!"

I reached the doors, shoved one open, and handed Lilly the candle. "Go!" She offered a grateful look and ran through. I was about to follow, when I heard a shout.

"Tony! Wait. You need to see this." It was my uncle Charlie's voice.

Force of habit—how else can I explain my idiotic response?—made me stop and turn about.

Uncle Charlie, along with Mrs. Penda, came out of the school office. Between them, they were holding up the Penda Boy. Or what had been the Penda Boy. He dangled from their hands like an old and dusty rag, like some little kid's toy animal, its stuffing gone, limp and lifeless. He had been seen, caught, destroyed.

I took a few steps toward them, away from the school's front door. "What did you do?" I cried.

"No more than he deserved," said Mrs. Penda. "He won't interfere anymore."

As she spoke, the reception hall gave a ferocious quake. With a roar, the stairway on the right collapsed. Wood, plaster, and brick tumbled. The hall filled with a billowing cloud of thick dust and debris. Simultaneously, great chunks of chandelier dropped and shattered, leaving only a few blinking lights, like the dying embers of a fire. Behind me, rubble cascaded from the ceiling.

I spun about and found the front doors blocked by a high mound of splintered beams and brick. I looked to where Mrs. Penda and Uncle Charlie had been standing. When the steps collapsed, they had retreated some paces into the school office. I turned toward the remaining stairway. It was still intact.

There being no other way, I shot forward and tore up the steps.

By the time I reached the second floor, Mrs. Penda and Uncle Charlie were following.

Not knowing where else to go, I ran down the hallway until I reached the end, Batalie's room. It was in complete disorder: desks and chairs overturned, books and papers scattered, computers tumbled. The SMART Board had shattered.

I peered down the hallway. Mrs. Penda and Uncle Charlie were coming fast, Mrs. Penda limping more than usual. I bolted into the classroom, but having nowhere else to go, I went to the small door that Jessica had already opened. I darted through and plunged into the hallway, only to realize it was now too dark to see. The best I could do was make my way by touch and memory. I had no real idea where I was going but knew that Mrs. Penda and my uncle Charlie were coming after me—wanting to kill me.

After no more than thirty steps, I became so confused I forced myself to stand still. Even as I did, the building shook with greater ferocity than before. Thrown against a wall, I fell to my knees. A complete section of the wall dropped away. I heard it crash, somewhere. Then, after a blast of cool air, I realized I was looking out at city lights and the moon. It was an outer wall that had given way. Below, I could see flashing red lights and screaming sirens. The school was collapsing.

As the whole school structure began to pry apart, sounds of creaking, breaking, and snapping surrounded me. Now the floor dropped at a sharp angle. I was afraid to move, terrified that more of the building would give way and take me with it.

I saw and felt the entire structure writhe, shift, and twist. Some walls heaved up. Others collapsed. With the floor so tilted, it was impossible to stand.

Somehow I managed to pull myself up. Moonlight provided some illumination. That allowed me to realize that I was high in the building somewhere. Half walking, half crawling, I moved toward a still-standing wall. Once there, I edged along its base, until I found myself in a partially enclosed area. Though it was darker, I kept going.

I found steps, which I managed to get on, and then worked my way down through a jumble of jagged, broken walls. I went across, up, then down again, but, having no idea where I was heading, I simply moved in hopes I'd stumble to safety.

At some point, at some place, I stumbled upon—and *stumbled* is the true word—that spiral staircase. I knew it because of the way it felt: cold, rough, metal steps and a banister, the steps twisting around, a mammoth corkscrew, still intact, probably because it was metal.

I put one foot on a riser. It held. Grasping the banister, I began to move down, only to hear voices coming from below. I halted and listened.

"I think he's up there" came Uncle Charlie's voice.

"You lead." That was Mrs. Penda's voice.

I peered below, hoping to see them, anything to tell me how far below they were.

"Don't worry," I heard Uncle Charlie say. "I've always been able to get him to do what I ask."

I reversed my direction and started going up, moving in tight circles through the murk. Now and again I reached out, hoping I'd come to a landing. I didn't find one, or if I did, I never realized it.

I halted and worked to find my breath, only to hear Uncle Charlie say, "He's above us."

Mrs. Penda: "Keep going."

I climbed faster and began to see light. Holding on to the metal banister, I continued upward. Gradually, I realized there was a hole above me. Only then did I grasp that I had reached the high tower, the very same place where I'd come upon the Penda Boy when I first spoke to him. It was precisely where he had told me *not* to go, because once there, I'd be trapped.

Though my ankle ached, and my heart pounded painfully, I continued to climb, trying to find some way to get away from my pursuers. That's when I heard Uncle Charlie's voice: "He's probably reached the tower room."

Mrs. Penda said, "Then we have him."

Having no choice, I moved higher, and was reaching up through the hole when the building gave another violent heave. The spiral steps, shrieking with the sound of twisting, breaking metal, fell out from under me. I began to drop. Using all my strength—the strength of desperation—I hauled myself up into the tower room. On hands and knees, I looked around. The floor was so steeply slanted I couldn't stand.

The Penda Boy's bed had slid to the far side of the room and flipped over so its legs were pointing toward me like a raptor's talons. The large window was empty. Glass shards had slid into a sparkling heap in a far, low corner.

I half crawled, half rolled toward the window. When I

reached it, I hoisted myself up. The tower had tilted down, even as other towers and roofs had shifted up *and* down. The building's roof looked like an ocean of crested and frozen waves.

One roof had risen so that it was right under the window. It seemed to stretch out toward that enormous tree. Farther below, a very long way below, was the street, where red lights were flashing. People were peering up.

I looked back over my shoulder just in time to see Uncle Charlie's lean face, with his pug nose, poke out of the hole.

"There you are," he called. "Now, Tony, you're not listening to me the way you used to. I just want us to be together like old times. It can be forever."

He looked down. "He's here. Can't go any farther." He began to hoist himself up, elbows jutting out like enormous spider legs.

Frantic to get away, I looked out the window, down at the connecting roof crest, which ran from the window to that tall tree. I was struck by how much it looked like a slackline.

I looked over my shoulder. Uncle Charlie was out of the hole. He was peering down. "Hurry," he called to Mrs. Penda.

I grabbed the edge of the window and swung one leg out and then the other, until I was sitting on the window's lower sash. Gripping the window's sides, I was able to steady myself and steal a quick look back in time to see Mrs. Penda's head rising up out of the hole.

I looked across the way, toward the great tree.

It's the same as a slackline, I told myself. *Just higher.*

Still seated, I set my feet on the roof crest, one foot in front of the other. If anything, the roof crest was wider than my slackline. It was solid, or at least it felt so.

Holding on to the window frame, I pulled myself up until I was standing. That meant the roof crest was holding most of my weight. Ordering myself not to look back, not to think of anything but what I was doing, that this was the only way I could escape, I told myself to let go of the window and walk.

I was standing on the roof crest, some two hundred feet above the ground. To either side of me was emptiness. Behind me lay the still-collapsing school building. Before me—a good ways off—was that old tree, as yet intact. Below were waves of jagged roofs, points, knobs, and broken chimneys. At the very bottom was the street—a long way down.

Trying to settle myself, I began to walk the crest as if it was a slackline. Arms stretched out to either side for balance, I was like a flying bird, though the last thing I wanted to do was fly. I just needed to walk the line from the dead building to that living tree.

With tiny steps, I moved forward.

"Tony," came Uncle Charlie's voice from behind. "Don't do it. You can't. You'll fall. You need me. You can't live without me."

Don't listen, I told myself. *Think with your feet.*

Once, twice, three times, I paused to find my balance, my breath, my nothingness, before I could proceed. Small step by small step, I made my way, drawing ever nearer to that huge tree, which somehow seemed to move farther away from where I was.

I think I was three-quarters of my way across when I heard crashing from behind. The roof crests—unmoving before— now began to heave and sway. Now I *was* on a slackline. If anything, it felt more comfortable, so much more like the wobbly walk I had always taken.

Just think with your feet, I told myself again.

Five feet from the tree, the shaking became so extreme that I ran the final distance and made a dive at the tree, grabbed a branch, and clung to it as the roof crest fell out from under me.

I was still hanging from the branch when I heard massive

splintering and crashing sounds. I looked over my shoulder in time to see the entire Penda School break apart and collapse upon itself with a great *whoomp*.

I swung a leg up, curled it around the branch, and, rough though it was, pulled myself toward the bulk of the tree, where I nestled against its great trunk among inner branches. There I clung and looked back toward the Penda School.

Nothing was left but a great mountain of rubble, over which dust hovered, a thin, drifting cloud. The weather vane, the angel Gabriel, lay twisted and charred. Licks of flame fluttered about it, like little dancing demons, perhaps truly dying ghosts—what remained of Mrs. Penda and her terrible friends. And yes, Uncle Charlie too.

I was still in the tree when a huge ladder rose up from the ground and came at me. At its top was a fireman, clad in a helmet and a yellow jacket. Weird but true, his yellow jacket reminded me of the one Lilly had worn that foggy day, when she invited me to her birthday party and I began to learn the truth about Jessica.

The fireman guided me to his ladder. I was soon out of the tree and on the ground amid an applauding crowd of fire-fighters, police, and people who had come to watch.

Two of the people were my parents. "Tony!" cried Mom, engulfing me in a hug. "That was amazing."

Dad also hugged me for a long time, and whispered, "Thank God Uncle Charlie gave you that slackline so you could do that."

I was home. As soon as I was alone, I called Lilly.

"Oh my God," she said. "You saved my life. I can't believe all that, can you?"

I said, "What happened to Ms. Foxton?"

"They say she's in the hospital. I guess she'll be all right. Tony," she added, "where are we going to go to school?"

I said, "Someplace normal, I hope."

"Tony."

"What?"

"I'll never go to another Halloween party."

Later that night, I looked for my uncle Charlie at the foot of my bed, where he used to appear so often. When he didn't, I have to admit I was relieved.

I lay there, tired but very much alive, more so than in a long time.

I thought of that quote from Albert Einstein: "The distinction between past, present, and future is only an illusion."

Maybe.

All I know is that I got out of bed and finally began to unpack the boxes of junk I'd brought from back east. It was time for my future.